I returned, and saw under the sun, that the race is not to the swift, nor the battle to the strong, neither yet bread to the wise, nor yet riches to men of understanding, nor yet favor to men of skill; but time and chance happeneth to them all.

Ecclesiastes 9:11-12, KJV Holy Bible

ToyShelf Services LLC
Presents

OUR
love
DIVINE

TOYA RAYLONN VICKERS

ToyShelf Services LLC

Special Dedication

When I first started writing this book, I did not know that my paternal grandmother, Etoyle, suffered from a mental health disease. It broke my heart to know that. Yet, to hear about how she passed was devastating. At that very moment I knew the relationship that I had with my immediate family members would have to be mended delicately, sympathetically as well as earnestly. I had to totally forgive and give them over to my Lord and Savior Jesus Christ. I love them dearly, but I must continue with my life, keep my faith, as well as the joy, peace and love that God gives to us freely and without conditions. So, to them, my dear biological sister and father, I give you this book to let you both know that God is Love and He loves all of us. Let us each carry our surname with dignity, integrity, and graciousness.

Introducing and Coming in Fall 2024

Vickers & The Associates

Advocating, Building, & Serving the Community Extensively

Acknowledgements

First and foremost, I give all my honor, praise, and worship to God, Abba, the Father who is the head of my life. The Holy Bible says "seek ye first the kingdom of God, and His righteousness, and all these things shall be added unto you." Found in Matthew 6:33. Since spring 2019 I have been in a battle. My ex-husband began hurting me physically after years of emotional, verbal, and financial abuse on top of his infidelity. I couldn't take it anymore, so we got divorced in January 2020. Then Covid devastated the world in March 2020. To really make matters worse my mother started falling frequently anywhere and everywhere with no warning or reason. I had been seeking God's kingdom, doing what I believed was right, why was I being tried by fire, Lord. I learned sometimes the fire is sent to purify you for the next level.

Raylonn Cookie Cox Smith was my mother, my Mama, my truest best friend, and the matriarch of the Cox family line of Clarence and Rachel L. Cox. She passed away on June 20th, 2022, at 9:11 pm from an extremely rare form of Parkinson's disease called Progressive Supranuclear Palsy. The horrible disease took over the part of the brain that controlled her limbs and eating. By the time she succumbed to the disease, she could not walk, barely moved, ate, or drank. I was her caregiver from 2018 until the Lord called her to Him and her spirit left the earth realm. Yet I know to be absent from the body, is to be present with our Lord and Savior Jesus Christ.

My heart is still broken but mending as I am living and walking in faith tending to the purpose given to me by the God of Abraham, Isaac, and Jacob. Before she passed, I answered the call to minister and gave my first mini sermon on Good Friday in 2022 at New Birth Christian Ministries in Columbus, Ohio where Kenneth Moore is my Bishop and Yaves Ellis is my Pastor in Ohio. Shaking and nervous, I stood in front of the congregation reminding them and myself that our God will never leave us or forsake us found in Matthew 27:46. Mama was too weak to attend but my sister, Zoe Vickers, made sure she could watch it at home. I want to thank both Bishop and Pastor as well as Elder Vincent Coleman, the community at New Birth, especially God's Ministry for Women with Minister Lawana Christian as lead servant, for helping in molding and all around uplifting me while learning how to minister to the people. Bishop Moore your teaching, preaching, and reprimanding was necessary for me to move forward. Please do not ever think that I left because of "church hurt." I moved to Texas because my heart was broken, and my disease was trying to manifest itself again due to my grief. Again, I am so very sorry about your loss too, yet your wisdom and advice helped me keep going and know that God still loves me, especially in this grief.

Now, I live in Garland, Texas taking the steps I needed to take, particularly with the disease of the mind that I was diagnosed with long ago. Trusting, believing, and having faith in God, Jesus Christ and the Holy Spirit I stand believing in You dear Lord. Today I am a member at One Community Church where Dr. Conway Edwards is our lead Pastor and Dr. Herman Baxter our Garland campus pastor. I started serving before I joined to be a member or committed to pay my first fruits in tithes.

At this point in my Christian walk it is not about me at all, because I am saved and have been baptized at Triedstone Missionary Baptist Church. Now my assignment is all about introducing Jesus Christ to as many people I can before He calls me home to glory. By giving a true word from the Bible to edify them, telling them my personal testimony of how He loves me, and then asking the key question: Do you believe in Jesus Christ? The people the Lord assigned to me are victims of child abuse, human trafficking, and mental health diseases. So, if you wanted to know what and where I have been, Dr. Toya, as the princesses of the night started calling me, I've been in the trenches serving as an evangelist, one of my actual spiritual gifts. I have been about serving in our communities for people who are usually forgotten, thrown away and treated horribly by despicable people. God has given me the strength, power, and courage to meet them where they are at, on the streets, not to far off from where I was in my colored past.

To that end, I want to thank some very key tribe members who sharpen me as much as I sharpen them from Proverbs 27:17. I pray you will always be salt and not sugar, you each make me better as we fly higher like the eagles. Senora Jelks, Marisa Sherrod Gillum, Stephanie Smith, Delores Cox, Denise Jarmon, Therza Douglas, Mary Murphy, Sharon Snow, Joylynn Ross, Tanisha Stewart, Pastor Uncle Steve Cox and last but certainly not least Diane Cox Buchanan.

Also, to my favorite one from day one, he's been protecting me since I can remember and does not play about his little sister/niece,

Adrian Lamont Cox. Uncle Ace, thank you for being there for me whenever you could. Thank you for always being a mirror making me check myself before I open my mouth to check somebody else. I thank God for you, your life, your heart, and the love you have for all of us in the family. Please continue to do what you do as it is necessary for you to do it. I finally figured it out, they want to play chess even though I most times play Russian Roulette, so I don't have to deal with the aftermath. That's toxic and unhealthy so I'm choosing to grow up and be accountable. You are up to bat next. Write the book, Unk!

To end these acknowledgments, I want to say to my cousins, please pay attention to more of what I say and have taught you, especially from the Holy Bible, no matter what has happened to me in the past or will happen in the future. Because none of those matters, I am covered by the blood sacrifice of Jesus Christ.

I love you all. May God continue to bless you and keep you because He is still a miracle worker, a healer, and loves us just as we are. Selah.

Contents

ONE

Old love made new.

Regina's Story

As the handcuffs fell from my hands and feet the doctor told me to sit on the couch in front of me. It was our weekly session, another hour or so, where I would tell him my truth and hopefully, they would let me out of this hellhole. Here came that doggone nurse with that shot. He looked at me from across his resolute desk. I gave Mr. President the same debriefing that I gave to my superiors.

Innocently enough, my man and I met one first Sunday while our Pastor was beginning to preach. Mama and I arrived late, yet for some reason she wanted to sit in the middle section instead of our regular seats on the left side of the sanctuary. I sat next to a handsome young man I never laid eyes on before, which was weird because I had been attending for over ten years. No sooner than I sat down, the young man jumped out of his seat and started shouting. He shouted a good shout too, and Pastor stared at him. He was all by himself, then, just as quickly as he jumped up, he sat down, overcome by the Holy Spirit.

I patted him on his back and said, "God is good," and the Holy Ghost shot up within me and I jumped and started shouting too. Now everyone was looking at us like, *what's going on with you two?* Pastor said, "Oh my, my, my, my," and laughed.

That was over twelve years ago. He had one more year to propose, or I was done with this mess. We dated for three years after we met then decided we should just be friends. It was frustrating because he told me I was his ideal woman. That was within the first six months of our courtship. I started falling in love with him; however, the feelings were not mutual enough for us to sustain a serious romantic relationship. So, we became friends. Over time, my love waned, and I grew fond of another man and got engaged. When I told him about my engagement, he said he had to call me back because he needed a drink. That relationship lasted almost a year until I found out the man, I wanted to marry was a thieving, conniving, cheating liar.

Fortunately, I escaped that den of deception a little hurt but wiser. I stopped letting men in and started working on myself. As I worked on myself and my relationship with God, I watched my friend grow into a well-versed minister. While we were dating, we never had sex and he said it was because he wanted to wait until we got married. Then there were the rumors that he was on the down low, but he continued to profess to me that he was indeed heterosexual. I found out that he was in fact into women when we finally could not hold our lust for one another any longer and succumbed to the flesh. It was exhilarating. To me, he was powerful, he was special, he was the truth, he was Jeremy Marquis Spencer. But that was two years ago. We rekindled our relationship after a ten-year hiatus.

It had been several days since my thirty-sixth birthday when I got the shock of my life. He called me to give me birthday wishes and ask me out to dinner. I agreed because we were friends and I missed him. As I was sitting at the restaurant waiting for him, I checked my Facebook page to see all my birthday wishes and comments. I scrolled through them effortlessly until I got to his post. He said, *Happy Birthday! I love you and I hope you have a wonderful day.* I wasn't surprised by the words *I love you* from him because we had already solidified that we loved each other in a friendship kind of way. What I was tripping on was the fact that he declared it in front of thousands of people on my page. I started to wonder, what in the world was going through his head now?

He showed up five minutes later and we hugged as usual. He sat and poured his heart out to me. He confessed that he had been naïve to let me go so many years ago and he was now trying to make sure he solidified what we had. He told me I meant the world to him and that I could never be replaced. He grabbed me by the hand and looked me dead in the eye and said, "I love you Regina and I can't live without you." I had a blank stare on my face but finally got the words out.

"What does all this mean, Jeremy?" I tried my best not to get excited.

He didn't waste a beat. "It means I want us to start over and begin loving one another the way we do and build it into a love so divine that Satan himself cannot touch it."

Why in the world did he say that?

"Are you asking for us to be a couple again?" My heart raced.

"Yes Regina, would you be my lady?" He was still holding my hand. I thought to myself, *Girl, you finally got him!*

"Yes, I will be your lady." We went on eating our dinner and laughing and having an enjoyable time. It had been a couple of days, and I had a chance for it all to sink in. Now I realized my mistake. I should have given him the ground rules so he would know I wanted to get married before I was forty, which meant getting engaged by thirty-eight. I had time to get this information to him and let him cop out so I could be available for the man who was really supposed to be my husband. Who was I kidding? I had been dreaming about this man being my husband for over a decade. The Lord already told me after I fasted and prayed for days about our relationship that he was attached to my spirit and that the Lord would cultivate our relationship. Satisfied in that truth, I had been waiting but I was tired. Keisha called my phone.

"What heffa!" I shouted at my best friend because she was starting to irritate me. The repeated calls of her complaining about her crazy mama and her antics were getting on my last nerve. But I had to be there for my best friend because she'd been there for me in everything.

"My mama is getting crazy about this menu for my wedding. She thinks that just because she is paying for it, she can do whatever she wants. This is my wedding, Regina; doesn't she know that?" She sounded frustrated. I had been hearing about this situation for the past couple of weeks and I was getting tired of it.

"Girl, you need to put your foot down and let Mama know this is your day, not hers. Let her know you appreciate all she is doing for you, but she has to let you express yourself in your one and only wedding."

"I don't know how she thinks she can dictate what we are supposed to do at our own wedding. She is so full of it, I swear. Then my cousin is tripping and talking about how she can't afford to pay for her dress and that I should pay for it."

I looked at the phone and decided I would listen because she already heard my opinion about letting her crazy cousin be one of her bridesmaids. Tonight, Jeremy and I were going to the movies, and I needed to put something in my stomach because those snacks at the movie theatre were too expensive. He would still get some popcorn and pops though; I knew him and most of his vices. I forgot Keisha was on the phone when she started yelling, "Hello?"

"Oh, I'm sorry girl, my mind was somewhere else."

"You were thinking about that man again. All I gotta say is don't get your hopes up too high. You know his track record. He ain't all that."

"I know but prayers have been answered."

"I'd give that fool six months and if I don't get a ring, I would be moving on for good and ending the friendship because that is too much nonsense."

"This coming from the girl who moved in with her man after only four months of dating him."

"I got my ring three months later, didn't I?" she said proudly.

"Yeah, that is true." I remembered how he surprised everyone, especially her worrisome mother by proposing just three months after she moved him into her condo.

"Patience is a virtue, but you have taken it to the extreme. Give that man an ultimatum before the end of this month so you will see exactly where it is he wants this to go." She made her final statement.

"Okay, I think I'll take your advice." First, I would ask Mama and my other best friend who were actually married though. "Girl I'll talk to you later."

"Alright, have fun boo." We hung up. A couple of hours later, Jeremy and I went to the movies. We had fun as usual then he wanted to go downtown to the waterfront and take a walk. We walked and talked and then I got the courage to say what was on my mind.

"Jeremy, you do know I want to get married."

"Yes, I know sweetie. I am not going to string you along, I promise."

"Yeah, but still though, I think if we set a time for us to make this official, to at least get engaged, it would settle my mind a little. We have been friends for a long time, and I know you say you want more and that's what we are working on but I'm thirty-six years old and I want to be married before I turn forty." I stopped walking and sat down on a bench. We watched the water glisten under the moonlight. He sat next to me as we discussed the elephant in the room.

"I understand what you're saying. I think I can put your mind at ease by saying this. I am not just trying us on for size. I'm trying us on for life. I want you to be my wife for the rest of my life." He grabbed my hand then kissed it. I looked at him and everything within me wanted to believe him, but I was unsure. I looked out at the water and wondered what I was getting myself into. The beautiful full moon sparkled as it got a little nippy for this time of year. I looked at him again.

"I don't know, Jeremy. Why do you suddenly want a relationship again? Is there something you are not telling me?"

"Regina baby, there is nothing I haven't told you that I need to tell you. I love you. I have for years now."

"But are you in love with me passionately like a man is supposed to love a wife, not just jovially?"

"I am in love with you, Regina," he assured me.

I looked at him and we kissed passionately. We sat there and talked some more about our relationship and future. Then he took me home and we kissed again like we were teenagers at the front door of my apartment. When I finally got into the house, I stood in the doorway and watched him drive off. I began to question God.

Father, what is it that this man really wants? Is he the one? Settle my heart and give me peace about this thing. You have the final say.

TWO

Thick as thieves

Keisha's story

I couldn't believe we were getting married. I knew he was the one but after he lost his second job in less than nine months, I didn't think we would ever get here. Now he had the position he said he had always wanted and if I could get my mother to get off my nerves, this wedding would fly off without a hitch. Isaac Lampley and I met through eHarmony. He was refreshing to say the least. I loved the way he scratched his stomach after he stuffed himself silly and played in my hair while we slept. I couldn't believe we were getting married. I said that almost every day.

In about three months I will be somebody's wife. I didn't know if I was ready yet though. I read some books on how to be a good wife and a lot of them were about compromise. I knew how to compromise;

I just didn't like to. He could be a handful, especially when he was under the weather. He could also be a brat. One time he had a simple cold but acted like he had the bubonic plague. The man had on three pairs of socks, two pairs of pajama pants, two thermal tops and a sweater then had the nerve to say he was sweating too much. Well of course, fool! You have three layers of clothes! He also had the heat set to hell because his mama said he needed it to beat the cold.

The only real complaint I had was sometimes his work ethic could be a bit off. I didn't think he realized since he was the newcomer, he had to suck it up and put his ego to the side. He had been through several jobs since I met him. At least four. Each time he thought his bosses didn't value who he was, a Black professional man. He didn't swing across the trees to prove himself to anybody. But he loved his new position and it had been going well for the past couple months.

But I had a madwoman in my way every doggone day, my Mama, who got on my last nerve. She thought that just because she was paying for our wedding, she could make all the decisions. I wanted chicken, she wanted fish. I said chocolate; she said lemon meringue. I said no to thirty people; she said they all need to be there. It was like pulling teeth making every decision along the way. I thought I would get to enjoy this time with my soon to be husband, planning our big day, but no, not with my mother standing in the way all the time.

If I could start this all over again without her I would. The only one I could depend on to not give me any headaches was my girl Gigi, otherwise known as Regina. I loved her to death. We had been best friends since the second grade. She beat up Clarence "Rockhead" Claytor for pulling my hair and throwing dirt in my face the first day of school. That girl knew she was a tomboy back in the day. She would play football with the boys, play in the mud, shoot BB-guns and everything.

I was glad she turned into a flower around tenth grade. When we were growing up, we treated each other like blood sisters. No one could separate us in high school either. My dad used to call us "thick as thieves" all the time. When he died five years ago and I had to get Mama to put the bottle down, Regina was right there with me. When I had my miscarriage in undergrad at TSU, she was there. And even though she couldn't stand the pink and green she was there with all kinda paraphernalia when I crossed the burning sands for Alpha Kappa Alpha Sorority Incorporated. I wished I could talk her into becoming a member, but she said she would spit fire and brimstone first.

We were going to the dress fitting in about ten minutes. I saw her pull up in her Impala bumping some Fred Hammond. She got out of the car with her shades on trying to be cool.

"Hey Gigi, I'm over here!" I yelled from my Infinity parked in front of Alfred Angelo's on the west side of Columbus. It was the middle of the afternoon, and the sun was shining bright.

"Wassup girlie? How are you? Get out and come on so we can get this over with."

I got my butt out of the car, and we hugged and walked into the shop. Vanessa, the stylist, was there waiting on us and greeted us with all smiles.

"The gown is gorgeous. You are going to love it, Keisha. And your dress is wonderful too. Where are the other girls?" she asked with her eyebrows raised.

"They will be here within the hour. I wanted some time alone with my maid of honor first."

"Well, you will be in the big dressing room. I'm going to go and get all the dresses now." Vanessa walked to the back of the store.

"Okay, what is going on? Why did you want me to meet you before everybody else?" Regina asked.

I let loose, the words flowing from my mouth like a river. "I have reached my limit with Mama. She had the nerve to tell me the colors need to be changed to create an atmosphere of elegance, as if that had anything to do with it. We got into this big argument, and she basically told me that if I wanted to see any more money from her, I better get with the program. If Daddy were here, I wouldn't have to put up with this bull-crap. He left ten thousand dollars specifically for me to get married and she has been holding it over my head for months. She changed the venue three times and I had to threaten her to put the deposit down to keep the last one at the Kelton House. I don't think I can take any more of her mess." I threw my hands up in surrender.

"Okay, I think I have a good solution. Call a meeting with her and Granny Barb and let's see how much more mess she will be able to come up with. You know Granny Barb can put her in her place and she ain't gonna stand for all of this because she loves you to death and wants to see you get down the aisle," Regina said intuitively.

"Girl, I swear, you always know what to do. I forgot about Granny Barb. My mom can't stand daddy's mama, but she will obey out of respect. Thanks girl. Now let's see how this gown looks on me," I said as Vanessa came back with the gown in her hand. She took it out of the bag, and it was phenomenal. I started to cry. I reached out and touched the satin fabric. It felt like silk and the jeweled embellishments made it even more stunning. "Oh my God, I'm getting married Gigi. I'm getting married." She gave me a hug and then we started getting me into the dress. It took a good fifteen minutes just to lace up the corset.

"Aw, you look absolutely gorgeous. It's so beautiful girl. Lil' Keisha is getting married," Regina said, smiling from ear to ear. I looked at myself in the mirror and melted. Even though I had been arguing with Mama I wished she was here to see it again. She was there with us to pick out the dress, but I couldn't take anymore of her silliness this time. I took a picture of myself with my camera phone.

"Okay it's your turn. I see Denise coming from the parking lot." I was looking in the mirror in the middle of the store and saw her coming. My cousin knew she could stand to lose a couple of pounds but nobody could tell her any different. She walked in with Vivica following her. Her daughter looked nothing like her. She didn't get her bubbling frame nowhere and had long hair like her grandmother.

"You look fabulous!" Denise said, walking through the door. Vanessa saw that as a sign to go and get the bridesmaid dresses. We hugged and fussed at each other while Vivica played around in the other dresses.

"Are we going to be the most beautiful bridal party to do it this year or what?" Regina said, walking back into the dressing room with her dress. Just then Patreece came in and Vanessa gave her the last dress. Patreece was Isaac's sister. She was a doll. She was a Delta, but everyone couldn't be perfect.

"Hey Keisha, I'm here, did you already try on your dress?" Patreece asked while stepping into her dressing room.

"Yes girl, I'm getting out of it now, but I took a pic of it. It just needs a little tightening and maybe a slight hem, but other than that it is wonderful." I stepped out of the gown from behind the dressing room walls.

"Shoot, I tried to get here on time so I could see it, but a pic will do. Ours look great too. I lost a couple pounds to make sure I can get into this size twelve because they said they run a little small. How is everybody doing?" Patreece asked while trying on her dress.

Everyone answered her as they got into their dresses. They walked out one by one and each one had a problem with their fit. The dress did run small because we got Denise a size twenty-two and it still didn't fit her, and she wore an eighteen. We all got re-measured, and the seamstress made notes for each dress and then we went to lunch at Mongolian Barbeque. We had a ball. After that, I went home to be with my Teddy-bear. He looked so cute standing in front of the stove trying to cook some spaghetti.

"Hello dear," I said, dropping the keys in the bowl on the corner next to the door of the garage.

"Hey baby, how did it go?" he asked, stirring some sauce. Looking too good with that apron on and a tank top on. I could see those big muscles moving while he cooked our dinner.

"It needs to come in a little and a simple hem and it'll be ready. What have you been up to today?"

"Looking at the game and fussing with your Mama. That woman knows she can't stand me. How in the world am I ever going to get on her good side if she won't even try to have a decent conversation with me? I mean really." He stirred the pot. It smelled good with the garlic permeating throughout the house.

I kissed him and put my arms around him. "I'm gonna fix her. I'm calling Granny Barb on her. She will get her together for the both of us."

He kissed me again and squeezed me real tight then smiled wide. "Good, now maybe I can get some peace. She called talking about some darn flower arrangements for the venue and asked if you picked out the right ones. Now she knows I don't know anything about that, but I think she called just to fuss and see what I was doing. She's a trip, Pookums." He shook his head.

"Wait a minute; I already picked out the flower arrangements. Did you tell her where I was?" I asked with concern.

"No, you told me not to tell her you were at the dress shop trying on your dress because you did not want to have to explain to her why she was not invited." He spoke proudly, knowing full well if my mama showed up at the dress shop there would be furniture moving by the time they left, and she would be banned from the store for life.

"Good, where did you tell her I was because I turned my phone's ringer off on purpose? She must've called you when she couldn't get me." I tasted the sauce and winced a little. "Baby, did you season this at all?" I started chuckling.

"Yeah, babe, I swear I did." He was proud of his little dish.

"What salt, pepper and garlic only?" I asked, teasing.

"Yeah. What, that's not enough?" He was totally unaware.

"No dear, let me school you." I got out the spices and hooked it up. We got the dishes out but decided to wait to eat. We sat on the couch and watched the rest of the game and cuddled with each other.

Then we turned on some music and sat at the table to eat. We tried to sit at the table at least once a week just to feel normal.

His daughter called after dinner fussing about her little brother and wanting to know what she was getting for her birthday. Her stupid mother, Loretta, was being a witch and wouldn't let the kids be in the wedding. That was one of the simplest women I ever met in my life. She claimed they didn't need to participate in the wedding because our marriage will not last more than a year and that he was just using me to get back on his feet.

Truth be told, she wanted him back, but they had been divorced for almost six years. She needed to get the hell over it and get her own man. I almost went off on her last week when she sent them to the house without any change of clothes. She knew we were going to his family reunion and wanted to throw a monkey wrench in our plans. Little did she know I wasn't afraid to take care of her kids.

When I finally met them, it was kinda strained because their mother had been telling them all kinds of stuff about me being mean and unkempt. It took a good three months for them to be okay with coming and staying over. His daughter, Angela, was so cute. She knew she had her daddy wrapped around her little finger. I couldn't wait until we had our own set of two. I wanted exactly two kids, a boy and a girl, one for me and one for him. When we had them, he would have a total of four kids.

I knew it was a lot, but we would be able to manage. He made sixty-five thousand a year at his job. I could pull in a good forty myself if I taught at my school during the summer or did something to supplement while being off from the main school year. I knew as soon as we got married that heffa ex-wife of his was going to demand he pay child support and put him on papers. She said that as soon as he told her we were engaged.

I didn't care. God had provided for us throughout this relationship, and I had never seen the righteous forsaken nor his seed begging for bread. I wasn't worried about a thing. We were just making sure mama didn't sabotage our wedding plans. The monthly counseling sessions with our pastor had been going well. We didn't have any underlying boobie-traps that we couldn't get over.

Isaac was a gem. He had a degree from Ohio State University in computer science and was earning an MBA from Keller. He combined them to get the perfect position for him as an online executive for JP Morgan Chase. When he got the position and started working, he came home one day shouting. I was happy he was finally happy with his job. Now he had a career position where he could grow and take care of our family for years to come. My phone rang and I wanted to ignore it, but I knew I couldn't get through this day without a call from Mama.

"Hello Mother."

"Now you're answering the phone. You do know we have a crisis right now." She was making a mountain out of a molehill for sure.

"Pookey told me something about the flowers. Mama, I told you we wanted the roses and calla lilies. It matches our theme for the wedding. Red roses too, to match his accessories." I rummaged through the box with the wedding favors that still needed to be assembled. All of a sudden, I got a crick in my neck, and I knew it was nothing but stress from this woman on my phone.

"I thought you said you weren't sure about red. It is just so, I don't know, basic," she said, thumbing her nose again at my wedding scheme.

"Mama, when did you get married?"

"Girl, back in 1972!" She spoke proudly.

"Did you have the flowers you wanted for your wedding?"

"Of course, we had everything we wanted for our wedding. Your father…" She began her lengthy list of accolades from my father, but I cut her off.

"Mama, I want roses and calla lilies; that is, it, short and simple. Now let me be, I have to get ready for church in the morning."

"Fine, I'll let them know and finish the order. Good night sweetie. I still love you despite everything." She was trying to be funny.

"I love you too, Mama." We hung up and I went into the bedroom and snuggled up under my man. About an hour later I got up and sat out our church clothes and took my weekly candlelit bubble bath while listening to some Maxwell while he slept and scratched his unmentionables before I came to bed.

THREE

If only for one night

Jeremy wanted to have dinner at his house tonight. I decided to wear a nice simple dress and cute heels, not too sexy though. It has been about two and half months since we started dating again and it had been wonderful. We talked every day, even if we were just saying hello and checking in. Every week he took me out at least twice and at church, if he was not in the pulpit, he sat with me. The other single women at the church who had been putting themselves out there waiting for him to bite had been giving me the evil eye. One of them, Cassandra Means, had the nerve to bump me a couple of Sundays ago then turn and look me up and down. Jeremy saw it and kissed me on the cheek. It felt so good.

Here I was at his condo. Now all I had to do was keep it simple and not be too flirtatious even though I did want him to try something.

As I rang the doorbell, I could hear him fumbling around. His eastside condo was quaint but spacious on the inside. The green door and off-white siding were a good combination. The lilac bush he planted ten years ago still flourished every year and smelled so good. He opened the door.

"Hello, sweetness." He reached out for me to come in and gave me a hug and kiss.

"Hey babe, you smell good." I smelled the scent that seduced me early in our relationship. He had on my favorite Burberry cologne. He knew that made me melt in his arms. Now I was flustered but in a clever way.

"I hope you like steak, T-bones to be exact. I got some broccoli and garlic potatoes with a nice Chardonnay. You ready to eat boo?" He led me to the dining area. There were candles lit and with the smell of the food there was another aroma that made the whole atmosphere feel enchanting. He even had some Luther Vandross playing in the background. The man also had the nerve to have on a shirt I bought him and some slacks and nice shoes. Now I felt like I should've dressed a little sexier, but he didn't seem to care.

"I love it babe, the food smells delicious but what else is that I smell?"

"Vanilla amber scented candles. You like?" He smiled proudly. Then he sat me down on one of the chairs at his grandmother's antique dining room table then went into the kitchen and brought out our plates. He went back and got the bottle of wine and poured it then he said grace over our meal. We ate quietly, only making small talk and giggling with each other. After dinner he went into the kitchen and came back out with slices of cheesecake. I knew he cooked the dinner, but I had to ask.

"Boy did you make that or are you perpetrating a fraud?" I giggled.

He looked me dead in my face and said, "Baby, I got this recipe straight from Sarah Lee." Then he burst out laughing. He was so silly sometimes. But the cheesecake was good. He stood and reached for my hand and led me into the living room. Prince's *Adore* was playing. He took me into his arms, and we started dancing. It was nice dancing with him and holding him. We danced to about three songs then I had to excuse myself to the restroom. When I came out, he was sitting on the couch.

"What are you thinking about babe?" I asked, moving to sit next to him.

"What movie you might want to watch. How about your favorite, *Love and Basketball?*"

Of course, I was obliged, and we sat and watched the movie while snuggled together. He would place little kisses on my neck and blow in my ear which was titillating. When it was over, he turned back on the music and brought candles into the living room. He got down on his knees in front of me and took one of my feet into his big hands. He then started to massage my feet and crack my ankles. It felt so good. I got a little excited from it too.

"What are you trying to do to me sir?" I asked because I was feeling it now.

"Come down here and look me in my eyes."

I moved to the floor with him trying to be as coordinated as I could in my dress. I had on pantyhose and of course they ran while he massaged my feet. We sat there and looked deep into each other's eyes and held hands. He started to move in closer to me and then he kissed me, and I almost exploded. We kissed fervently and then started to move our hands over each other's bodies. He palmed my breasts through the dress, and I started to unbutton his shirt. I couldn't believe this was about to happen, but I couldn't stop myself. I wanted to make love to this man so badly.

We took off each other's clothes slowly but purposefully, stopping to look at what was revealed. When he got down to my undies he stopped. He was almost naked with only his boxers on, and I could see him full grown through the cotton. He stood up and lifted me, carrying me into his bedroom. He laid me down and finally uncovered my beauty and his. We made passionate love to one another for hours that night and in the morning had a quickie. When it was all said and done, he leaned over and said, "I love you so much. I don't think I'm gonna be able to live without you."

I looked at him and there was a single tear coming down his face. I cried too. We held each other for a while and then I got up, asked for a T-shirt, dressed and went into the kitchen. I cleaned up our mess from last night and made breakfast while he showered. When he came out, I had breakfast waiting for him in a tray and we ate in the bedroom. I showered and put back on my dress. We talked and laughed like an old married couple. Then he said something that made my heart jump.

"When do you want to get married, Regina Belle Watkins?" He waited for me to respond. I stalled for a couple of seconds.

"I want to be married by the time I'm forty, which means I'd like to be engaged within the next year or so."

"That sounds doable. What would our marriage look like, dear heart?"

"I think it would be full of love and respect, and a lot of compromise and communication will be essential. We will have our own separate careers but always make time for each other. I think you will be an elder within the next five to seven years and I will be able to deal with the responsibility of being a preacher's wife. I believe we would be together through sickness and health until death does us part," I answered while trying to figure out what to make for lunch. We continued the discussion for about an hour then changed the subject to something less heavy.

I left his house around three in the afternoon. I went home and cleaned up a bit and started to daydream about what our lives would be like when we got married. I prayed and asked for forgiveness for last night's lust, but I knew it would probably happen again because I could not get enough of him. I took a long hot shower and then took out my clothes for work the next day and fell asleep. He called before I laid my head on my pillow.

"Goodnight sweetie, sleep tight and don't let the bedbugs bite."

"Goodnight love." I fell into a deep peaceful slumber.

The next day was a mess. It took me a while to get to school, because of course people couldn't drive in the rain in Columbus, Ohio. There were two accidents on the freeway on the way there. Then once I finally got there one of my students got sick all over the place. I wanted to call his parents and give them my two cents but instead I sent him to the nurse and let her deal with it. Then it was a trip trying to get the class to settle down after that. Everyone kept talking about how bad it smelled and how they were starting to feel sick too. Then of course someone really did get sick, and I had to stop class again and deal with them. It wasn't until after school that the nurse said that there was a stomach bug going around and to try to keep all the kids separated as much as possible which meant no sharing food or drinks.

When I got home, I was feeling a little queasy, so I took some Pepto and laid it down early. I had to get up early in the morning and grade papers. Glancing at my phone, I saw missed calls from Jeremy and Mama. I called Mama at six because I knew she would be up.

"Hey Mama, what are you doing?" I asked, still trying to grade papers.

"Girl, you know I was sitting here reading the word. I heard you and Jeremy have been getting reacquainted. What's going on with you two, Regina Belle?" Mama asked, being nosey.

"Well, we started dating again seriously and I think it may just go the distance, Mama. He asked me about getting married and what our marriage would look like and everything. I think he is serious. We even made love." I swallowed hard because I knew I had said too much. A bead of sweat trickled down my forehead as I waited for my mother to give me the business.

"What you guys have been falling into is lust with each other. Humph, yeah, he better be talking about getting married. You ain't no whore of Babylon, you are a Ruth. He better come correct or I'm going to get him. You know I almost got him after the first time, remember that. You were such a mess after that. I can't see you go through that again, ever. Your Daddy has been asking about you too. When are you coming by?"

"I want to come by Sunday after service. Are you going to cook?"

"I guess I could cook a little something, make a pound cake too. Clarence would love that. Let me go though, I got one more chapter to read and then gotta make some eggs and bacon for your father before he gets on out there." She was rushing me off the phone.

"Mama, where do he be going? He does know he is retired right? He's seventy-five, ain't he tired?"

"Girl, you know better than that. Clarence has been working since he was ten. He doesn't know how to rest. Plus, I think he's scared to stay home too long with me. We haven't been newlyweds in decades." She giggled.

"Mama that was way too much information. I am getting off the phone on that one. Have a good day."

My parents had been married for over fifty years. They got married young. He was only twenty and she was seventeen. They didn't have me until they were in their thirties. She had a couple miscarriages and they had stopped trying when I popped up. After me, she couldn't have any more, so they were happy with me. I had the same problems she had and couldn't have any children. When I was in my early twenties, I had three miscarriages and the last one messed me up so badly inside the doctors said it would be a miracle for me to conceive again. I told Jeremy that when we started dating and he took it well. Still though, I worried about him not being able to carry on his namesake.

FOUR

All I do is think of you

Kiesha

It was time for us to take our engagement pictures and send them out with the invitations. Tomorrow I will have a meeting with Mama and Granny Barb to put an end to all of Mama's mess. We were going to Franklin Park to do the pictures. I loved the conservatory and the gazebo. If we had enough money I would have got married there but since Mama was acting up we would get married at the church and have the reception where I wanted to be in the first place, Kelton House. Isaac said, "Are we really gonna have it there or does your Mama have something up her sleeve to throw at us down the line?" I reassured him that the deposit was made and all we had to do was complete the menu.

While we were at the park we walked and talked hand in hand and the photographer took videos of our time together. We talked about how we met, avoiding the eHarmony truth and perpetrating the fraud that we met at the mall, and he followed me around until finally getting the nerve to speak. We talked about our first fight when he was late picking me up for a date and didn't call. I refused to go out with him for three weeks after that and he was livid. He came over to my house one day out of the blue with groceries in hand and made me dinner by candlelight. I let him back into my good graces after that.

After the photo shoot we went to Red Lobster and ate really good. I had so many butter bay biscuits I could hardly finish my real food. We sat there for two hours enjoying each other's presence and the atmosphere of the restaurant. He wanted to go to the steppers set after, so we went and danced the night away. When we got home, we wanted to be with each other but were so tired we passed out in our clothes.

Today was the day of the infamous meeting. We were meeting at Bob Evans so there wouldn't be any craziness and plenty of witnesses. It was gonna be a showdown at the O.K. Corral today. I picked up Granny Barb and we went on ahead to the restaurant. When we got there of course Mama was nowhere to be found for fifteen minutes. She finally showed up overdressed.

"Hello Mama." I stood and received her.

"Hey Pumpkin." She gave me a hug then hesitated and said, "Hello Mother Barbara," as warmly as she could.

"Hello Delores, you look well put together today for Bob Evans." She took a shot at her.

"Oh Mother, you know I have to be fierce everywhere I go." Mama looked at her with a pretentious smile.

Let the games begin. We each ordered our food and ate and chatted for a bit, then Granny Barb opened up the topic of discussion.

"I hear you have been giving my dear granddaughter a rough time as she tries to plan a wedding so she can be happy with the man she loves."

"Why do you say that?" Mama, of course, was not going to readily admit that she had been trippin'.

"Let's talk about why it took you so long to pay the deposits even though my son set ten thousand dollars aside for this blessed event. It's not like you don't have the money. Why are you giving this girl hell at every corner?"

"Did she tell you that he has been fired from two jobs in less than six months and the one he has now only made pennies?"

"What does that have to do with anything? When you and Daniel started off, he was only making eighteen thousand dollars a year and you were pregnant. He ended up making over sixty-five thousand at his job because he moved up the ranks with promotion after promotion. At least the young man is taking care of business, from what I hear," Granny Barb countered.

"Oh really? Living with his girlfriend for a year and a half paying when he can be taking care of business?"

"Mama, I am his fiancée now and he has always paid his way. I don't know what you are talking about." I was pissed.

Granny cut back in. "Look, it doesn't matter. They love each other and are getting married. Delores, you need to stop putting wrenches in their plans just because he isn't one of your frat brothers with an expense account somewhere. Money and love are two different things that should never stop one from developing a life together. My beloved Anthony was a poor man, but he loved me to riches. Stop all this childishness. I mean, really." Granny Barb wiped her mouth with her napkin. That was the sign that the discussion was over, and she started going through her purse because she needed a mint.

Mama sat there looking like a scolded child and I was eating it up. We said our goodbyes and I took Granny Barb home. She told me something valuable again in the car.

"Baby girl, money will be there forever, but love doesn't come to everybody. If you really love this man, dedicate your life to loving him good until death do you part. Okay honey?" She kissed me on my cheek. I loved my Granny Barb; she always had some wisdom to put out for me to grab onto. Now I had to stop by Gigi's and tell her about the showdown.

As I was driving over there, I called Isaac to tell him I loved him and give him a quick rehash of what happened. He started cracking up laughing and said he would have loved to be a fly on the wall to see Mama put in her place. I then called Gigi to make sure she was home and tell her I was on the way with the news. She said she had something big to tell me too. Oh Lord, what was going on with my girl now?

I got to her house, and we went straight to the couch and turned on some Jill Scott, fixing some grape Kool-Aid mixed with Simply Lemonade. I told her what happened, and she fell out laughing.

"I told you Granny Barb would get her together. She loves you like you are her own daughter, and she knows that Auntie can be on a trip. But she sat there like a scolded child pouting for real girl? Dang, I wish I could've seen that. I know you wanted to shout and laugh too." Regina laughed.

"Girl yes! Mama just sat there with a prune face because she knew she couldn't say anything back. She had the nerve to throw out Isaac's finances as the reason why we shouldn't get married. Granny Barb quickly reminded her of how her and Daddy started off with a baby. I was like, for real. Mama always made it seem like I came a long time after they got married." I sipped from my glass.

"Wait, what? You are lying!" Regina said, cracking up.

"Girl yes! Delores Renee Mosley has been perpetrating a fraud for years. I heard that was the only reason they got married but she always refuted that assumption. But yeah, Mama had a shotgun wedding. Ms. AKA and all."

"Well, it doesn't really matter if they loved each other to death. But girl, I gotta tell you something." She smiled from ear to ear, looking invigorated.

"What is this big news you have for me, because girl, you look like you have seen heaven or something. I mean your whole aura is full of light." I stared at my friend's glow. Her skin was smooth and supple, her eyes glistened, and her smile was contagious. She looked like she had kissed the sun.

"Jeremy and I made love again. And girl, he put it on me. I have never felt that way about a man before and afterward… Girl afterward, he said he couldn't see himself living without me and asked when I wanted to get married." She started giggling like she used to when we were teenagers, then we talked about how we were finally getting the men we had always dreamed we would be with. I just hoped that this love spring would continue to flow.

FIVE

Don't be shy.

Regina

Today, Jeremy wanted to go watch baseball. I thought we were going to see the real players but instead he took me to the park over by Greenlawn where all the youth leagues were playing. I instinctively felt a tingling in my stomach. We went over to one of the areas in the back and sat in the stands. He brought water for us and started cheering for somebody named Little Jeremy. Now I was getting nervous. We had missed most of the game and saw the little boy score the winning home run. The little boy then walked up to us afterward and said, "Hi Dad! Thanks for coming. You were late though." The boy hugged Jeremy. I was speechless. This boy looked to be at least six or seven years old. I had to be dreaming. Somebody needed to slap me back to consciousness. Jeremy hugged the boy who was his spitting image and kissed him on his head then he turned to look at me.

"Regina, I would like you to meet my son, Jeremy Jr. Son, this is my girlfriend, Regina." I stood there, flabbergasted. I thought I was going to faint and couldn't get any words out.

"Nice to meet you Ma'am," Junior said shyly, then held out his hand to shake mine. I shook his hand but in total silence. I couldn't believe what I was hearing.

"You guys want to go for some ice cream?" Jeremy asked, then nudged me. I put a smile on my face and finally gathered the strength to say, "Sure! Nice meeting you too, Junior." I looked him over. There was no denying it, this was Jeremy's son. He was the spitting image of my man. The same man who never told me he had any children whatsoever. I smiled politely and immersed myself into the conversation until he dropped the little boy off. As soon as he got back in the car, I tore into him and smacked him.

"How could you?" I shouted, totally undone. Tears streamed down my face, and I started heaving like a big baby.

"Baby, I'm sorry, I was going to tell you the night you came for dinner, but one thing led to another, and I didn't want to ruin our night together." He said this like that was a good enough excuse.

"That boy is six years old. You should've told me when he was born." Then it dawned on me. "Wait a minute, we were together six years ago. You bastard! You cheated on me. That's the real reason you couldn't be "in love" with me like you said. You were cheating on me. How could I be so blind? Oh, my freaking God. Take me home right now." I refused to say anything else to him. So many thoughts were running through my mind. When we got to my place, he exited the vehicle and tried to open the door for me, but I jumped out of his car and started toward the door.

"Wait Regina, baby we need to discuss this! Everything is okay. It's just that I have a son we can both love." He tried to grab onto me.

"No, no, no it's not that darn simple. You omitted an excessively big part of your life from me for over six years. You don't respect me and you for darn sure don't love me. Is that why you wanted me back because she broke it off with you? Is that really the reason, Jeremy? I'm second best?" I opened the door to enter my house. He pushed the door and tried to follow me in, but I slammed the door hard, almost trapping his fingers in it. I locked it. He tried to open it then started knocking on it as hard as he could.

"Regina, it's not like that. I love you and I want you to be my wife. Please baby, don't do this. Please!" He shouted and knocked for fifteen minutes. My neighbor got tired of it and called the police. When he saw the patrol car, he left upset. I was still sitting in front of the door and felt and heard every knock and word. But I couldn't get past this. I was just on top of the world and now I was in the valley.

He said he wanted our love to be divine. It was almost as if God was telling me that could never be. But why couldn't I have something I deserved? *"Why Lord why? I've followed your commandments, I go to church, and I volunteer my time in the community. I'm a good woman who searches after righteousness and yes, I did have sex with him, but I've been abstinent for almost three years. This was not fair. Why are you doing this to me now? How do I deserve this mess? I love this man! How could he do this to me? A son, a six-year-old son? Darn it to hell! How could I trust him after something like this? He's kept this from me for six years, why?"* I shouted out loud. *"Lord, I don't know what to do now. Why would you give him to me only to take him away because I don't know if I want him anymore after this?"*

I slept for two days and missed a day of work. When I finally got out of bed, I felt so defeated I called out another two days and stopped answering my phone. He called every day at least a dozen times. This mess had shaken me to my core. Everything I thought about this man was shattered and torn apart by his lies. I was angry for believing in him and loving him so much, then pining over him like an idiot.

All I did was love this man. He could have told me the truth years ago. Maybe I would not have remained so enthralled by him and could have made myself available to other men. Not me though. Like a teenager who didn't know any better I sat around and kept one foot inside his circle just in case he picked me. What in the world had I done? I needed to talk to someone; maybe Mama. No, she would just say *I told you so*. I didn't want to call Keisha because all she was gonna say was, *I told you so too* and I didn't need to hear that right now. I didn't have any other close friends who would listen and not judge. Stephanie might have but she was at work. I cried some more, realizing how small my inner circle was. I went into the kitchen and ate the last of the Grippos chips and another ham sandwich with grape Kool-Aid. This turned out to be too much to handle. I put on Karen's first album and tried to get out of my funk, or at least functioning well enough to take a shower and clean my funky room.

I gave in and called Keisha when I knew she would be home from work and free. After I told her about the horrid event, she sat there in silence for a couple of minutes and then said she was on her way over. I let her use her key because I had gone back into my room. She came inside and gave me a big hug and let me cry hard and scream and say whatever came to mind. Then she sat me down and told me I had some decisions to make regardless of him having a six-year-old son.

I owed it to myself to talk to him about it and figure out if I was ready to give up on a love, I harbored for almost a full decade.

I hadn't thought about that, a full decade of loving him. There were so many ups and downs, I could make a rollercoaster ride out of it. Was he worth it? I couldn't have any children, and now he had someone to solidify his future as a man. Was that so bad I couldn't forgive him? I didn't care. I wasn't ready to talk to him about it yet. Keisha put a lot of stuff into perspective for me. She never said "I told you so" either, which helped tremendously. I was surprised that she said I should try and work it out. We talked about it almost every day now.

"Girl, I don't know why you're acting like you are not going to give that man what he wants and been wanting all these years. Quit playing coy and bag him."

"What? You think I should try to work it out with him?"

"I mean yeah. Look at me and mine. We kept going despite the adversity we faced. We kept faith in God and each other and your girl will be married soon." She always said Jeremy was too good to be true. Guess she was right.

I was going to work in the morning. Being in the classroom and looking at those little faces would uplift my spirits. I refused to talk to Jeremy though, maybe in a couple of weeks.

SIX

When a woman's fed up

Regina

let two weeks go by before I answered his phone calls. He called
every day - at first a dozen times, then he got down to three. He sent
flowers with nice cards four times and came by a couple times. I was
home but acted like I was not there when I saw his car in the driveway.
One time he sat on my porch for two hours waiting. I felt sorry for him
that day and sat in the window looking at him through the curtain. I
wanted to hug him, but I had to put my foot down. This was not going
to be easy. Letting him get away with this mess was not an option and
I was gonna make darn sure nothing like this ever happened again.

The first call was simple enough. He asked, "Is it over?"

"I don't know. I have not made up my mind yet. You need to give me the time to figure things out." We sat on the phone for a good two minutes before he spoke again.

"You sound so good on the phone. I miss your voice. It has always been soothing to me."

"Well, I'm busy at the moment." It was a lie. I was hoping he would try again later. He called four hours later. "Can I come see you? I miss you so much."

"Not yet; I don't want to see you right now."

"Have you made any decisions yet?"

"Not yet." My head started hurting. This time we sat on the phone listening to each other breathe for a while. He finally said, "I love you Regina and I am not going to let you go easily, not over this. I know I messed up. I should have been man enough to tell you about Junior when he was born but that was my idiotic mistake. I have done so many things wrong toward you and I promise I will spend the rest of my life making it up to you. Please sweetie, give me another chance to prove to you that I am the man that you deserve."

I listened to his spiel but still wasn't convinced. I told him I needed more time. He said to take all the time I needed, and we got off the phone. The next morning there was a basket at my door with all my favorites in it that he must've made himself and brought over. There were Now & Laters, Grippos, Grape Kool Aid, Dark Chocolate Raisinets and some roses inside, among other things, as well as a handwritten love letter. He could be attentive at times. I have to admit I was a bit fed up, but I liked all the attention.

Work was hard that day too. The kids would not pay attention and kept acting out. I had to put one in the corner a couple of times because he wanted to shoot spitballs at all the girls. I could see him being a ladies' man when he got older. All the ones who pulled hair and did stuff like that always end up being big flirts.

When I got home, there was another gift at my door. I opened it and it was a homemade CD of all the songs he knew I loved and a poem he wrote to music at the end. The poem made me tingle. I saw now he was not going down without a fight. Still though, I was a bit fed up, but I liked the attention. I was in the house less than thirty minutes before he called. I let it go to voicemail and started fixing dinner. I thought about maybe dating other people for a little while, just to make sure this was what I wanted. Let him see that I was a hot commodity. That might backfire though, he was a Taurus. Here he was on my phone again.

"Hello?"

"Hello dear, how was your day?" he asked.

"It was a lot of work at school. The kids would not get settled and I had to put one in the corner a couple of times. Other than that, it was productive." I was cordial with my response.

"That's good, sweetie. What did you cook tonight?" I could tell he was hungry from the way he asked.

"Some chicken breast, rice and green beans with some sweet, iced tea from Turkey Hill." I waited for him to invite himself over.

"Sounds good. I'm going to BW3 with the fellas tonight to watch the game. Wish I could come over though." He sounded sincere.

"I don't know if I am ready to see you again. I have been thinking about everything and it's not the fact that you have a son that upsets me; it's the fact that you kept it from me for all these years. That bothers me. Especially since that is something so important to your life. I know you say you and the mother are not together but that is unimportant, it's that you didn't respect me and our friendship enough to tell me about your son. That was messed up. I feel betrayed."

"I understand. There is no excuse, Regina. I don't know why I couldn't bring myself to tell you the truth. There were times I wanted you to be there so badly, especially when he was a baby. I missed you really bad and wanted to see you hold him, my seed."

"Well, it is too late for all that. I guess in retrospect at least you do have a seed because I can't have children. Maybe that was one of the reasons you did not want to say anything because you didn't want to throw it up in my face. Still though, the secrecy is something I don't understand and will not be able to get over any time soon."

"Can I suggest something?"

"What's that?"

"Do you think if we went to counseling, we could work this out? What do you think?" He sounded hopeful.

"I Dunno, who could help, I guess. It would not hurt but I am not saying yes right now. I still need time, Jeremy. Please don't make this harder than it already is with a lot of calls and pop-ups; that is not going to make it any better. I do like the gifts though. They have been thoughtful at least. I'm about to work on tomorrow's list and get ready for bed soon. Okay."

"Okay." We hung up the phone. I knew he was still gonna call like he was on crack though. Sometimes he didn't listen. He might still pop-up too, but I wasn't answering the door when he did. I had so many feelings about this situation. I knew I couldn't have kids so I was glad that he had someone who could carry on his name.

However, I didn't know how much it would have hurt if he told me six years ago. I could have held his baby. I could hug his son now, but it was not the same as holding him as an infant and smelling that baby scent on him. That would have been the closest I would ever come to him having a baby I could hold. What was I talking about? I could get a surrogate. But he couldn't have actual sex with her. Why was I even thinking about that? I should be moving on, but I couldn't. I loved this man. He was everything I ever wanted. Yet this transgression was a big one. Maybe counseling would help. We could put everything out on the table. At least I knew he wanted this to work and possibly be my husband. That was all a girl could ask for.

I needed to pray about this. Lay prostrate before God and travail about it. I hadn't done that in a while. It was time I did. I would be able to see him and not smack him in another two weeks or so. Until then he needed to be on his best behavior. If he did anything else, I didn't know what I was going to do. Men were a trip sometimes. Why couldn't they just do what they needed to do to keep the woman they wanted and not get into any shenanigans? That would be too right though. I still couldn't believe how Keisha was raising a banner for our love. She knew how I felt about Jeremy though. I wouldn't be right if we were to break up. That man was in my pores, and I secreted his love every day.

I needed to pray about this. I got up and went to the living room and laid prostrate before the Lord. I couldn't get my words together at first and just cried. The Word said He would bottle up every tear. Just then, I found the words and asked first for forgiveness and then discernment into what it was He would have me to do. I told the Lord exactly how I felt, betrayed, and defeated. I asked Him again if Jeremy Marquis Spencer was the man, He had in store for me to marry. I then laid quietly and waited for His response. I heard Him whisper to me the story of Rachel and how she was barren but in time He opened her womb and she bore Jacob's son Joseph who was the dreamer and became dear to the pharaoh. She was a woman that was very fair but at first could not conceive but God heard her prayers and gave her what her heart desired.

I got up after that and read the story and studied Rachel most of the night. I never understood the story or how she mimicked my life in a sense. I had the courage to finally call Mama. It was late and I knew she was asleep, but she could tell by the sound in my voice that something was wrong. She listened to everything I had to say without once butting in or saying something to upset me. Then she told me something that I thought I would never hear her say.

"Regina Belle, if you really love this man you have to accept him with all of his flaws

and faults or you will be doomed to a life of regret and unhappiness. With that being said, continue to pray about it, but I think you already got your answers. Just walk in what God has given you and don't be afraid of mistakes. Mistakes make you the person you are. You don't want to be with a person who can't admit they have made mistakes in their life. That person is not being real with themselves, you, and better yet with God. Know this, love is not promised to us. Only God can give you unconditional, unfathomably, unrelenting love dear, only God can."

I listened. We chatted more then got off the phone. I had a good night's rest that night.

The next morning, I woke up early and left the house. I decided to go to the park and take in the fresh air and feed the squirrels. I thought about how long I had been in love with Jeremy and if that was enough to carry me through. I thought about who he was as a man and what I adored about him. Right then and there I pulled out my little notepad and did a pros and cons about Jeremy. When I finally got done after about an hour or so, to my surprise, he had a few more cons than pros. That alarmed me for a second until I started reading and measuring each con versus pro.

For the most part he was a good man. I did love the fact that he was a minister and active in the church. I loved the fact that he did some volunteering for at-risk youth with his fraternity Phi Beta Sigma. I had almost forgotten he was a fraternity brother because he never talked about it unless he was with some of his old college buddies who were still active. He didn't pay attention to it anymore but when he was in school, he said he could stroll with the best of them. Then there was the fact that he did have a child.

That was something I had to sit and ponder seriously. I did like the fact that he had someone to carry on his name; however, I wished I had known about his son as a baby. Still though, I knew about him now and could make up for lost time. I didn't know what I was fronting about. I was going to stay with this man. He was the best thing I had going for myself in the relationship department in a long time.

That last fool Adrian Matthews was a heathen. He had the nerve to try to take me there, even stealing from me. When I finally got him out of my life, I prayed to God to never put me through any mess like that for the rest of my life. I was in a place where I didn't love myself enough to say no to anybody trying to pursue me. I should have known it was going to be a bunch of crap when he took me out for the first time and then asked me for twenty dollars to help pay the bill. If a man started asking for money your first time out, he was a loser, point blank period. I didn't care if he was only asking for fifty cents.

Still though, Jeremy had my heart. I loved this man, and he loved me. I would try counseling to see what happened. I hoped we could work through our issues enough to make this relationship better. If all else failed, we would learn something about each other and our relationship dynamic. It was starting to get cooler, and I'd been outside for three hours. Tomorrow would be a new day, and God willing, the worst was over.

SEVEN

A Mother's love is undefined

Keisha

Our Pastor felt that we were doing well in pre-marital counseling except for all the mess my mother had been bringing into our relationship. He asked us to bring her in for one of the appointments and she agreed. Today we would be able to face her as a united front, one couple in love, no matter what. If she loved me, she would stop all this nonsense and be happy for me. Even though we had a meeting with my Granny she still found ways to cause friction. Pastor felt that it may have been her way of hanging on to her little girl. I didn't think it was that simple.

Isaac didn't think she respected him at all. He was not cool with that mess either because he thought she would try to undermine everything he tried to do for our relationship to work. I kept trying to reassure him that I was not a Mama's girl. I loved her, but I could do without her suggestions. My dad was a great man, and he had some big shoes to fill but Isaac was my ideal man, not because he had money and status, but because he loved me unconditionally.

It was less than ninety days before our wedding. I couldn't wait to be his wife. I would finally be official and not living in sin as Pastor put it. When we told the truth that we were living together he let us have it. However, he understood the situation and respected our decision. He said it was hard for any couple these days to live separately and move into marriage naturally like back in the day. Everyone was in such a hurry. Still though, the ones that did live together sometimes stayed together longer as far as he saw. He attributed that to the couple already knowing each other in and out before the wedding. Oh Lord, here came my mother, overdressed as usual.

"Hello, you two!" I stood to greet her. Isaac also stood and tried his best to be cordial. She recognized it but still acted funny toward him by turning her nose up and flipping her hair in his direction.

"Hello Mama, how are you doing?" I hugged her then got out the way so Isaac could hug her too. She gave him a half-hearted hug and we all sat and waited.

"What has Pastor been saying? Does he think you are ready for all this?"

"Yes, he says we are doing well and that we already had a lot of stuff worked out that he was going to make sure and touch on during the counseling." Isaac smiled.

"Oh, well let's see," Mama responded as the Pastor came out of his study and greeted us. He gave each of us a hug and then ushered us into his office.

"So how is the lovely couple doing this month?" He asked while taking out some paper and sitting down.

"It's been pretty good, I must say," I answered as Isaac agreed. Mama shifted in her seat, waiting impatiently to let loose the fire that she no doubt had been waiting to douse us with.

"And you, Sister Delores, how do you think the couple has been doing?" He asked her opinion but why in the hell did he do that? She was more than happy to let loose her flames.

"Well, I think that there needs to be more time for Isaac to develop as a man before he marries another woman. You do know he is divorced with two kids and his ex-wife still seems to burn a torch for him." She spoke matter-of-factly with a smug smile.

"I thought the ex-wife had moved on. It has been over five years since they were together, correct?" Pastor sounded a bit concerned now.

"It has been eight years to be exact, but there is nothing going on between us at all, sir." Isaac was pissed now and sitting on the edge of his seat as if he was ready to fight.

"But doesn't she still come around sometimes, and didn't you have to go off on her for trying to kiss you a couple of weeks ago?" Mama spoke with a smirk on her face.

"Mama, it was nothing like that and you darn well know it." I was pissed too now.

"That's not what you said when you came to the house crying and all distraught because you thought something might be going on between them. Keisha, tell the truth and shame the devil. There are still some things you two need to handle and you are not ready to get married, not to Isaac at least."

I could not believe my ears.

"Okay wait a minute, is there something you two need to tell me?" Pastor asked, sounding genuinely concerned.

"No Sir, my ex-wife tried to kiss me on my birthday. She tries every year, but since I have been in a relationship with Keisha, I have not allowed it to happen. She still has feelings for me and has had a tough time letting me go but I have not done anything to encourage her. She is just a lonely woman, but I have no feelings for her other than respect and admiration for raising our children." Isaac glared at my mother.

"Right, there is nothing going on between them and I know this. I have just been so emotional over everything that has been going on preparing for this wedding that I overreacted. I know he doesn't want her. He is in love with me. I also feel that I am ready to get married to Isaac no matter what my mother says or does."

"Okay so Mom, I have to ask: why are you so against your daughter marrying this young man?" Pastor asked.

"He is not good enough for her. Look at her and what she has to offer. If it was not for her, would he have a place to live? No. Would he be where he is financially? No. Would he be able to say he has everything he has been able to gather with or without her? Hell no! He is not worth the trouble, and he is just there because she takes care of him, not the other way around. He is not the man I see marrying my daughter." Mama spoke without blinking an eye. Isaac got up and in her face.

"You don't know anything about me except that I lost my job, and your daughter was kind enough to let me live with her until I got back on my feet. You don't know that since I got my new job over a year ago, every month I have been putting away the exact amount she spends to pay for a house to get ready to move into that we will both own. You don't know that I am the one she turns to because she can't tell you about some of her deepest secrets. You don't know that I pay child support for my kids every month and give them allowances. That I paid for that new car she has and the ring she has on her finger is paid off and insured. You have nothing to go on but stuff that happened over a year ago and you are jealous that she has someone in her life, and you are an old widow. You must be out of your mind if you think I wouldn't marry a woman who takes care of me and gives me what I need without worry or concern and who loves me unconditionally, something I never had even from my first wife. You darn right she is too good for me, but she makes me a better man and I would be a fool to not marry her." He stepped back, looked at our Pastor and said, "She does not have any say in what goes on from now on so with that you need to excuse her from this meeting. I have a life to lead with my soon to be wife." He then sat down and looked at Pastor.

Pastor looked at Isaac, then at me and then to my mother.

Mama was sitting there holding on to her pearls with a scowl on her face in disbelief. For once she didn't have a comeback for Isaac. He had finally put her in her place, and it felt good watching him stand up to her. I didn't know why but I felt flushed, and I knew my nipples were getting hard all of a sudden.

"I think Isaac has answered all the questions that needed to be answered from you. He is also correct; you do not need to be here, nor do they need your permission to get married. With that, I hope you can come to an agreement in the future, but they do not need you to be here for this. You can leave, Sister Delores."

"So that's it? Even though I have the final say over the final payments for this madness?" She had this devilish grin on her face like she just won the lottery and nobody knew about it.

"I knew you were going to do this. Delores, what you don't understand is Keisha is going to be my wife with or without your permission. This is the money for everything you have paid thus far. You don't have to worry about paying for anything else. I already have it taken care of." Isaac handed her a check for seventy-five hundred dollars. I looked at my husband and started to cry. A line had been drawn in the sand and I had to make the final choice.

"You're gonna let him talk to me like this?" Mama glared at me, standing. She was putting me in a place I didn't want to be in, but I knew it was always going to come down to me having to choose between the man I loved or my mother.

"Mama, I love you, but Isaac is the man I am going to marry. I can't stay single to please you and your backward thinking. He can take care of us as you can see. Please, just try to be civil toward him and I hope you still come to the wedding." I stood to hug her, but she inched away.

"You will regret this in the end. A mother's love can never be replaced no matter how much you try," she said disdainfully.

"This is what I was afraid of. Sister Delores, she is not trying to replace your love, just add to the amount of love she is going to get with this man. Please sister, don't ever feel like your love is being replaced. Am I right, Sister Keisha?" Pastor asked.

"Yes, you are right sir." Tears streamed down my face and Isaac held my hand. Mama looked at me and waltzed out of the room. We finished the session talking about ways to deal with her despondence and how to keep our love fresh and then said a prayer. When we got home, I cried hard, and he cried with me and then laid me down and made sweet love to me like he hadn't done since our first time.

EIGHT

One more cheap shot

Regina

We had been going to see Dr. Mars for a couple of weeks now
and to say the least it had been interesting. She had broken us
all the way down and was now helping to build us back up as a loving
couple. We were finally able to admit to each other that the main reason
we were back together was because neither of us felt we would find
anybody else who could or would love us or put up with us the way
we did each other. Basically, we felt as if there was no one else out
there that would be able to meet our needs and we felt that we found
what we needed in each other. She thought was a decent enough reason
to stay together but she understood how we came to that conclusion
together which was promising for our future.

She gave him the blues about Junior though. His decision not to tell me about something so important to his life screamed insecurity in his true feelings for me. I always thought that he didn't love me as much as he said he did, and when Dr. Mars reiterated my beliefs, he got upset. Still though, it was his actions that caused the issue between us which could be something that kept us from going further in our relationship. She suggested that we sit down and list everything we felt kept us together and what could tear us apart and come back together to compare.

When we got to her office we had to laugh because we both realized this could determine the success or failure of our relationship. We went through our lists back and forth with Dr. Mars interjecting to help each of us say exactly what we wanted to say to each other. Basically, as we suspected, we had some of the same things on our separate lists. He thought that having a son without me would make me want to leave him. I thought the same thing about not being able to have his child. He thought that that being a minister was one of the things that kept me with him and that was at the top of my list. I thought that he coming back after so many years was answered prayers. He said when I agreed to go to dinner, he knew God did indeed answer prayers. Dr. Mars said that spoke volumes and it would be beneficial to keeping us together in the future. She suggested that we keep our lists handy and every three months or so go back and adjust as needed. Our session went well, and I could see the light at the end of the tunnel. Tomorrow we are going out with Junior for lunch.

Junior's mother must have given Jeremy hell because when he came to pick me up, I swore he looked like he wanted to hurt someone.

"What's wrong baby?" I asked and waved at Junior.

"Nothing, well something, but I don't want to get into it right now. Do y'all want pizza or burgers?" he asked, then sped off.

"I want pizza," Junior said. He looked like he hadn't taken a bath today and his hair was bending over because it needed to be cut badly. I already knew what Jeremy was pissed about by looking at him.

"We're gonna make a couple stops first man, okay?" We rode in silence while he went to the mall and got him a couple of outfits and then to his barber and got his haircut. Lunch was late but it was cool, until his baby mama showed up out of nowhere.

"Come on Jeremy let's go!" She yelled, then looked at me up and down.

"Jamika, what are you doing here. I only told you where we were going to ease your mind. I don't need you to pick him up. I was gonna drop him off when we were done." Jeremy was annoyed.

"Well, you're done now. I gotta work tonight and the babysitter is all the way on the Westside. So, he got to go now. Get up Jeremy!" Junior just sat there like a lost puppy begrudgingly looking at his father.

"Look, I can take him tonight. I know it's not my weekend, but I really want to spend some more time with him and my lady."

"Look, you and this barren bitch can get him next week when you are supposed to. I got stuff I gotta do. Jeremy, if you don't get your ass up right now and get in the car, I'm gonna pop you upside the head."

"What the hell did she just say?" I was in total disbelief and utter shock. I was about to stand when Jeremy grabbed me by the waist.

Jamika cut in. "Look, just because you can't have your own kids don't mean you can take care of mine." She wore a smirk on her face and stormed out of the restaurant. Jeremy followed her and they started arguing in the parking lot. I sat there upset that he divulged something so personal to her of all people. I had enough of all these shots being thrown at me for no reason. When he came back in, I tore into him. He sat there for a second then told the server he wanted the check. He paid and got up to leave, totally ignoring what I said.

When we got in the car, he finally said something. "I did not mean to tell her anything about you. She started asking questions when she was pregnant, and I told her about your situation. I wasn't gossiping about you, Regina. I would never do that. I should have never told her anything about you at all but what's done is done. I do apologize, she should not have thrown that up in your face because she only did it to hurt you and start a rift between you and me. Please sweetheart, don't let her get her way," he pleaded, driving slowly.

"I don't understand why you would even bring it up. When we dated years ago, we never had sex and the only reason I told you was because I wanted you to be realistic about our future. I feel betrayed right now, yet again."

"Don't feel that way, sweetheart. It doesn't mean anything to me."

"Well now it doesn't. You have a child to carry on your name, but I will never be a mother." I held back the tears and let my hands grip my knees in defiance of my emotions.

"Yes, you will. We can adopt, remember?"

"Do you really want to adopt or are you just saying that to save face right now because you know I am beyond pissed?"

"No, I had been thinking about it before and I know when we get married, I want to share our love with a child. Wouldn't you like that?"

I started to daydream about a little one I could claim and who would call me "Mama".

"It sounds nice. But would you want a baby?"

"Whatever you would feel comfortable with. By the way, what size ring do you wear?"

"Stop playing; you don't want to know that right now out of the blue. You're just trying to make me feel better. Boy, you ain't slick." We chuckled and decided to go to the movies. Afterward, he dropped me off at home and gave me a kiss goodnight on my porch. When I got in the house, I called my girl Keisha, and we talked about the day's events.

"I don't understand why he would tell that heffa my business. That messed me up for the rest of the day. I started wondering who else he told and what they thought about me. Still though, he did say he wanted to adopt after we got married." I sipped on some Kool-Aid.

"Girl, he just needed to get it off his chest. That tramp probably wanted to see what she had on you and get ammunition and it worked like a charm. You never should have said anything while she was there to show that it bothered you. She's at home or work right now telling her girls how she got one up on you like it's really gonna matter. She needs to be worried about Jeremy taking full custody when y'all do get married, especially after how you said she had the boy looking today. Does she do that mess often?"

"I don't know, girl. But Junior looked like a hot mess. His clothes were nasty and too small. I don't know if he was clean, but we didn't have time to take him home and let him shower. Jeremy bought him a couple outfits and shoes and got his haircut. She did that BS on purpose because she knew he was going to go all out to make an impression on me. Little does she know, all this mess is going to backfire. When we do get married, I am going to put it in his mind to get full custody and adopt him."

"Right!"

"Right! Don't mess with me, heffa. How is wedding planning going? Are you ready? It's coming up soon."

"It's going well now that I don't have to go into Mama's purse. I didn't know my soon to be husband had been putting money away for this purpose just to shut her up. He amazes me sometimes, that's why I love him." She sounded so happy.

"I will probably be planning one soon. He asked me for my ring size today in the middle of the conversation about adopting." I snickered in delight.

"He really is trying to pour on the charm. I would wait until after all your counseling and stuff though. Just make sure he is the one, okay? You haven't been too impressed lately." That was the first time in a while she questioned our relationship. I wanted to know why but it was getting late, and I had to sing in the morning.

"Well so far, so good; he is the one I want to be with forever. But look girl, I gotta sing in the morning and need to get up early so we will talk after church tomorrow, okay? Love you," I said.

"I love you too girlie, goodnight." We hung up the phone. Jeremy called after I tied up my hair just to say goodnight and that he loved me. He could be sweet sometimes but when he messed up, boy did he ever. All I knew was I could not take any more mishaps. My heart couldn't allow it. I loved the man, but what did love to have to do with being respected and honored? He was supposed to do that as he loved me. That man could be a trip.

After work Monday, I wanted to have a conversation with him about everything we discussed in therapy. I planned to cook dinner and invite him over, no sex allowed though. He would be on punishment for at least a month for this mishap. A woman had to do what a woman had to do. Plus, we were in control of the sex in the relationship. It didn't get done unless we allowed it. I was taking my authority in this earth and expressing it.

Still though, love was not something that was promised between a man and a woman like Mama said. It was something that you had to work at every day. It didn't fall in your lap and allowed you to do with it what you would. Love was patient, kind and never boastful. It was full of compassion, kindness, and affection. It could be simplistic, or the most complex emotion ever felt. I wanted to give it to him as much as I could for as long as I could until the father told me differently and called me home.

NINE

I don't want to let go

Regina

Pastor was on fire this morning. We received a word from God and shouted really good. When the choir started with *Sweet Holy Spirit*, everybody got up and went in. He was talking about how God was the only one who could truly give us unconditional dying love. That He loved us so much, He gave His only begotten Son to us as sacrifice for our sins. He had started a new series on the love of God and today he started off with the special sacrifice of Christ. I was in tears thinking about it.

Keisha and I were meeting for dinner because we hadn't been out in a minute by ourselves. We decided to go to Max and Erma's, our old favorite. I remembered when the City Center mall was open, and we would go downtown to eat their wings. Now they didn't serve them anymore, but the food was still delicious. There was my girl at a good table. It was packed in here.

"Hey girlfriend, how are you this evening?" We hugged and kissed each other on the cheek.

"Girl I'm doing good. Isaac had the nerve to get a jealous because I said the dinner was for girls only. Had the nerve to sit there and pout like a two-year-old. He knows he can be a brat sometimes," she said as we sat down. We made more small talk, ordered our food and a couple of drinks and even started talking about the sermon again.

"I don't know if any man can ever love a woman unconditionally like God does. It is not in us to do that sort of thing. We always have something else to go with our love of one another," she started the discussion.

"I know. I am starting to believe that I will always come up short with the love I will get from Jeremy. He loves me as much as he possibly can, but the love that God has for me is so much more, no man can match it. That's why I have always been kinda leery when he says we have a "divine" love. Pastor said he is going to talk about that next week, and I got a feeling we are both in for a big surprise." I sipped my drink.

"Girl, you didn't tell me he was calling your love "divine". That's almost blasphemous if you ask me." She shook her head.

"I know, right." I nodded in agreement and sipped my pop. "I get so uncomfortable when he says it. But why he doesn't think or believe that it is, is beyond me. He tried to say he was meaning that it is the closest thing he can get from heaven and blah, blah, blah but it's just too close for comfort if you ask me."

The waiter arrived with our appetizers of chicken quesadillas and potato skins.

"All I gotta say is I know I don't have that with Isaac. And you know I can admit this now, in the beginning I thought he was just going to use me to get back on his feet and be done with me. I was already preparing myself for when he was gonna be ready to move out and on with his life. But when he came in that night with a ring in his hand I was floored." She remembered the night he proposed like it happened yesterday.

"Yeah, you came over the next day like you had seen a ghost. You acted like your Daddy had visited you from the grave and you had to tell somebody to make sure you didn't need to go to the looney bin. I was like what in the hell is wrong with my girl now. But then you showed me that ring and I was like alrighty now!"

"Yeah, I love Isaac, but I can admit now that he is not the man of my dreams, I thought I would end up with." She continued eating her quesadilla.

"Why do you say that girl?" I pulled the cheese off one too.

"He doesn't have his own stuff. House, car, etcetera, and like Mama said, he pretty much has been living off me which is why he has all this money saved up to finish paying for our wedding."

"Yeah, but he has enough now so you can put down on a house, right? And you did sell him your old car and put it in his name?"

"We don't have a down payment for the house anymore since he is paying for the wedding. He could've kept that money. I mean, Daddy gave me money for my wedding. Mama is just acting like a warden, and he got tired of it so just to prove a point he used most of his savings. We had talked about this before, and I hadn't realized he had that much saved up already. Now we're back at square one." Our entrees finally arrived. I didn't know how to respond so I let silence fall over us for a while as we enjoyed our food. She finally said something else.

"He doesn't want to have any more kids." She looked disappointed when the words came out of her mouth.

"What, wait? I thought you all had talked about this already?" I was concerned now because her life's dream was to have two kids, a girl and a boy, two years apart.

"I found out he had a vasectomy and never told me about it." She appeared to be shaken by the revelation.

I let that sit for a minute then said, "I take it this is what is making you question the relationship now."

"Yes! He is really not the man of my dreams, and I don't know how to handle not being able to have kids with him. I want kids of my own, Gigi. You know how long I've been planning for this stage in my life, since I was sixteen. And now, right at the beginning of my marriage, I find out my biggest dream will never be realized with him. We are almost done with the counseling with Pastor too. How am I gonna bring this up now?" She ordered another round of drinks.

"How did you find out?"

"I was cleaning up the office and found all this paperwork about it and a letter stating it was successful. But the point is he had this done three years ago. He could have told me this before he proposed to me. I feel like he set me up."

"Wow, I would never think he would do something like that. How long have you known about this and not said anything to him about it?"

"I've known for two weeks now. I keep trying to bring up having a baby and he changes the subject or avoids the topic. I think he knows I know because I didn't try to hide the fact that I went through the drawers in the office where he keeps his stuff. I don't know why he hasn't at least attempted to talk to me about it. I feel like he is keeping something from me, and he darn sure knows and doesn't care how I feel about it."

"Girl but you know that's not it. He is probably trying to figure out how to tell you. You know how men are, if they don't know how to fix something they don't try to deal with it. Just give him time and whatever you do, don't attack him about it. Have a serious discussion. But are you thinking about not going through with the wedding?"

"I am going to marry him, I'm just upset right now. I wanted to have a baby one day, but I am getting older, and he probably thought I didn't want any because I haven't talked about it with him before. Not seriously. But yeah, he is not my dream man, but I love him anyway. Yes, girlfriend, I am getting married." She smiled.

We continued the night talking about our men and how we had to admit the fact that they were not the men we dreamed of when we were little girls. However, who really found the man of their dreams? What you wanted and needed was the one of your reality because that was what you would be dealing with for the rest of your life. You didn't need a mate that you dreamed up and then it turned out to be something totally different from what God had in store for you. If God be for it, who then should be against it? All my life, He let things happen exactly as He has planned it so why fuss about it? I thanked God for a real man who loved God and wanted to be there for me. That was all I could ever ask for.

By the middle of the week Keisha and Isaac sat down and discussed children. He admitted he had had a vasectomy six months before he met her. He said he had decided that he was getting older and did not want to be in his fifties with a teenager. Keisha gave him an earful and then some. But then she said she understood why he did it and that it probably was best for them in the end. She accepted the fact that she would not be a mother, or that she would not give birth. However, being a stepmother to his children would suffice.

Jeremy and I had another therapy session with Dr. Mars and brought up the subject of more children. He reiterated what he had already said about us adopting a baby once we had been married for at least two years. I was happy knowing that he did want another child and that he was willing to go through all the hoops we would have to go through to adopt. Dr. Mars asked us about our parenting styles and what they would look like.

He was definitely going to be an authoritarian. I would be the peacemaker. We decided we were not going to pick favorites and make sure that our children were well cultured. He then said again that he wanted me to adopt Junior. I told him if and when he gained custody, I would have no problem doing that. We ended the session writing down some rules we were going to follow preparing to be good parents. She said the next time we met we were going to tackle how to argue with each other.

Afterward, we went out to eat at Texas Roadhouse. He loved their baked sweet potatoes and rolls. We were sitting there in our own world when his baby mother Jamika walked by the table with some man. Jeremy looked at her and she looked at him and asked how we were doing. The heffa stopped at our table and started talking to us like she never had any problems with us. She introduced her suitor as Mike, and he shook Jeremy's hand. Then they said their goodbyes and went to their own table. We looked at each other in astonishment and then Jeremy said, "What in the world just happened? Did she just introduce me to the infamous Mike? You know he's the major reason I want custody of my son, right?"

"No, you never told me about that. What's the problem?" I was concerned now because his whole demeanor had changed. He had sweat beads coming down his brow and his teeth were clenching.

"That man put his hands on my child so bad he ended up in the hospital. After that he hadn't been around anymore because I said as soon as I could find out who he was I was pressing charges my damn self. I'll be right back." Before I could grab him or say anything he got up and walked toward their table. Jeremy was talking calmly and then Jamika raised her voice. Then Mike yelled, "I think you need to go back to your table, partna. We tryna have a fun time. You don't want to end up hemmed up like your kid for disrespecting me." I got out of my seat.

"Fool, if you feel froggy then leap my nigga. Don't let the preacher's cloth fool you. Jamika knows what hood I'm from, partna." The next thing I knew, Mike hit Jeremy and they started fighting.

Jeremy broke a chair across Mike's back, but Mike broke a glass against Jeremy's head. Jamika and I tried to get them to stop but then she started calling me all kinds of b-words while she was at it. Finally, two guys got in between them, but it was too late, and management had already called the cops. We all got banned from the establishment and the police handcuffed Mike and took him to jail. Jeremy was full of anger which was a side of him I had never seen before. Jamika screamed expletives at us and then hit him when the police started to handcuff Mike. They didn't take her though because Jeremy refused to press any charges.

When we got back to my house, I listened to him rant and rave for another hour or so.

"I can't believe she is still messing around with that fool. He put her own flesh and blood in the hospital. She would rather have somebody laid up in her damn bed versus having a safe place for her son. I am through with that woman. I can't take this anymore, Regina. I can't." He finally stopped pacing enough and hollering for me to get a word in edgewise.

"Dear heart, you have got to calm down. I can't believe that you got in a fight with them while we were out like that. What were you thinking?"

"What was I thinking? I was thinking about my son sitting at Nationwide Children's Hospital with his arm in a cast because of that bastard! You know what? Never mind, because if I have to think about it again, I'm never going to calm down tonight." I made him some tea and got him to calm down until his son called. He had the phone on speaker, and I could hear Jamika running her mouth in the background, talking about how she was going to have somebody come after

Jeremy. Junior was hysterical on the phone. He had locked himself in the closet refusing to come out. She was kicking the door. Before I knew it Jeremy was out the door. I couldn't stop him.

I was on pins and needles waiting for him to call me back. Every time I called the phone went straight to voicemail. Finally, I got a call.

"Hello?"

"You have a call from an inmate at the Franklin County Jail. Will you accept the charges?"

"Yes."

"Hello, babe. It's me, Jeremy. Can you come and get me? I'm downtown. Jamika told the police I hit her, but my son told them I didn't and now they are saying I have a court date and can be bailed out for five hundred dollars. I'll pay you back tonight. Please come down here and get me?" Jeremy begged.

"I'll be there as soon as I can." Now I was on my way downtown to bail him out of jail. I didn't know if I was up for all of this. He never told me that he was dealing with all this drama in his life. But I saw why. This was a whole total mess. And if this was how this girl lived her life, we were going to be in for a fight if he wanted full custody. The problem was the whole fiasco today looked bad on him. He instigated the fight though Mike hit him first. And he went over to her house, so it looked like he'd been the aggressor in all this. *Lord, please, whatever you would have me to do here, tell me now so I can know how to help him.*

TEN

We had it all wrong

Regina

It was another Sunday morning at Corinthian and the pastor was preaching. He was still on his series about divine love and today he answered the question, *what is divine?* A lot of people had it confused, thinking God had to love us. But He didn't have to, He wanted to, and that was so much better. When someone wanted to love you versus having to love you, you are never an afterthought. You stay on that person's mind and they do things or abstain from things to show you one thing: that they love you. Divine love was even more special because it was the purpose of God to be divine; therefore, only He could give us divine love. What is divine? Divine is of or pertaining to God, heavenly or celestial. No one on earth could give you divine love because it came from God. Pastor Mills preached a good word today that fed my spirit and let my heart open even further to receive God's love.

After church, Jeremy and I went to the Cheesecake Factory and had an interesting conversation. He finally admitted he was wrong about how he viewed our love for each other.

"I didn't realize how wrong I was until this morning. I set us up for failure by letting those words pierce my lips. I'm sorry, Regina. I guess that explains why everything has been strained for us in this relationship." He stared into my eyes.

"I always felt bad after you said it or mentioned it but didn't want to correct you because I thought you knew more than me because you are a preacher. But after today and Pastor Mill's teaching, we know better. I guess God wanted to get us straight." We laughed a bit and then ordered our food. We sat and chatted more about the sermon and how awesome church was. He said he was going to do some more studying because surely, he needed it. He hadn't been preaching as much as he used to because he had been working more. Not studying every day was starting to show in his relationships.

"I want to ask you something," he said.

"Ask away."

"I want to start the process to gain full custody of Junior. When I get custody and we are married, are you going to adopt him as your son?" He asked this with this look of nervousness. I took a drink of my lemonade and thought about the question before me. A son, my own adopted son. It was better that he was his biological son too.

"Yes, I will adopt him."

He grabbed my hand and got up from the table to kiss me. He was so happy it was alarming at first. "Baby, why do you seem like you just won the lottery?" I asked him, smiling from ear to ear.

"Because I have. I already started the process of going up against his mama in court and I want you to be there through it all. I know we can't have children naturally but this way he will be our son." A tear came down his face.

"Aw baby doesn't cry. I would love to be his mother and your wife, as soon as you ask me." I wiped the tear from his face. We talked some more about having a family and what it would look like. We decided we would need to buy another house after we got married. Then he asked me if I wanted to go to the Bahamas for a weekend get-away. I said yes.

Later that day, I was on the phone with Keisha's crazy cousin. She called me, hysterical because her boyfriend gave her another STD. I didn't feel like listening again because he was always cheating on her. She allowed it to happen. All she had to do was break it off with the fool and leave him alone and wait for a good man to find her. Her problem was she had low self-esteem and didn't think she could do any better. I remembered feeling like that before I dated Jeremy. He was my hole in one and even though I did break up with him years ago it was the best thing to happen for our relationship and future. Now everything was going just as God planned it. His divine love allowed both of us to find each other again and given us a second chance. If it wasn't for His divine love, we wouldn't have looked at each other again. Still though, God let it happen.

That was the thing about His divine love for us. It made room for others to love us the way we wanted to be loved by man. If God did not love us the way He did, we would never find husbands or wives to be committed to. Without the divine love of God, the world would be a dismal place. There would be so much more strife and degradation to the point that you would expect trouble before peace. Without His divine love, there would be no peace on earth at all. There would be no joy. Yet and still, His love was all inclusive for humanity. That alone was so impressive.

The next day at work was a breeze. The students seemed like they were ready to learn and didn't let anything get in the way of that process. Even the little knucklehead, Barry Simms, was quiet and listening to every word I said. On Friday we would be sending them home with the yearly candy sale packages. The class whose sales the most candy won a pizza party. They were geeked about winning this year.

After work today I was going to go see Keisha and see what had been going on with her and Isaac. She said she was going to confront him about his vasectomy, and I hadn't heard head or tails from her since Friday. Now that I thought about it, I hadn't seen her at work today either. I hoped this was not a sign.

When I finally got to her house there was a box sitting on the porch full of stuff. I could hear them arguing from the steps. I knocked on the door and he came and flung it open.

"You need to get your girl, she is really trippin." Isaac walked out of the house. He picked up the box and went to his truck, got in and sped off. I opened the door and the house looked like a tornado went through it.

"Okay, let's start from the beginning. What happened?" I asked her while picking up the lamp on the floor.

"He lied to me. That nigga outright lied to my face even after I showed him the paperwork I saw. He claimed he didn't know how to let me know what he did. That he just doesn't want any more children and that maybe I don't really want to be married to him. I called that bluff, put his ass out!" She walked into the kitchen, fixed a shot of vodka then sat on the couch. I didn't know what to say because I didn't know she planned on doing all of this.

"What happened to the house?" I tried to make some room to sit in the Lazy-boy.

"He tried to take some stuff and I wouldn't let him. I paid for it, get your own sh…"

"Okay that's enough cussing. You are really mad at him girl. Are you ready to call off this wedding? You know what your Mama is gonna say."

"I told you so. I don't care. Why did he have to lie to me like that? If he would've just admitted what he did up front it would have never gone this far. Now I gotta go through with all this madness just to prove a point. Our wedding is in four months. He has to stay gone for at least a week or two just so he will know I ain't playing! Ugh, men they get on my damn nerves." She poured another shot.

"So y'all been in here arguing all weekend."

"Yup. I didn't let him in the bedroom, locked him out. He left Friday night when it started but came back in the middle of the night drunk. Had the nerve to bang on the door like I was really going to open it. Saturday, I found him on the floor in the hallway. Just to tick him off I started vacuuming at six in the morning. He woke up screaming at me, so we got right back at it. I left Saturday afternoon but couldn't find you and didn't want to ruin your day, so I got in touch with some old friends, and we had lunch. They both were like, 'You should have found out about this before he proposed.'"

"Right, he owed you that much respect at least. It was underhanded the way it was done. You all were dating when he had this done, weren't you?"

"Not seriously, but about two months before we got serious and six before he moved in. He knew he didn't want any more kids and let me daydream away like a fool. It seems like a set up to me for real. Like he was banking on me finding out and just going all the way the hell off. Like he wanted me to end it big time or something."

I got up to take the bottle from her.

"I don't know girl. Isaac is not that callous. He doesn't have a devious bone in his body, and you know it. Maybe it really was like he said. He couldn't find the words to tell you and asked you to marry him because he wants you to be his wife regardless. You know he loves you like a fat kid loves cake." I placed the bottle behind my chair.

"Girl, I don't know either. I was just in bliss a couple of weeks ago but look at me now. God sure got a lot of explaining to do." She forced a smile on her face.

We sat there and discussed all her options and listened to Isaac's begging on the voicemail. He was really trying to put his words together. He was staying at the Holiday Inn Express down the street from them on Hamilton Road. He was already complaining and talking about how he was hungry, and his back was hurting. He didn't know he had about a week or so to go before she would be willing to let him back in the house.

She had to make sure she hurt him for a while so he would know what he did was not right at all. She even started coming to terms with not having any kids with him. Maybe one day they could adopt. She was going to continue to work on him because she really wanted to be a mother. I had to remind her she would be a stepmother to his kids.

Still though, she didn't think being a stepmother was going to satisfy her wants. I was glad she realized that having children was a want and not a need. Everybody was not going to be blessed with the gift of children. She would have to take what she could get and be satisfied. Isaac loved her and he would probably take every chance he got making it up to her. I knew he would.

ELEVEN

If you want me

Now that Jeremy was doing everything, he needed to gain full custody of Junior, his baby mama was giving him hell. Since he had been paying child support all these years and FCCS had a case file on her, she didn't have a leg to stand on. The lawyer said as long as he continued to show that he could provide a better home for his son the judge would take all things into consideration. We were going to the Bahamas this weekend and I had been trying hard to find some nice outfits to wear. He said be sure to wear this off-white dress that I wore back in the day, but I hoped I could still fit it.

Keisha had been going through it with her fiancé. She finally let him back in but had still been giving him the business. She said she loved him and would go through it all again because she knew he loved and adored her. We were talking about my trip, and she said she thought Jeremy was going to propose so I should make sure I was looking fabulous every day. I told her he just wanted to get away because he had been stressed with work and the case but in the back of my mind, I did hope he proposed.

Last night we sipped on Chardonnay and listened to Miles Davis and compared notes. As friends we had gone through so much heartache and pain over the men in our lives but we both felt it was all worth it. I couldn't have children, but I was glad Jeremy had a son to carry on his name. I would feel some kind of way if I married him and couldn't give him a namesake. I was horrified when I first found out about Junior but now, I was using my head and letting my heart take a seat. A woman had to do that these days or she would end up angry, bitter, and cynical in all relationships.

I knew my mom would be a little upset but still happy for me. I missed Daddy so much and wished I could hear his voice one more time. I had a tape of him singing with the Kings and he sounded so good. I also had videos of them at their last anniversary party. My parents loved each other even though they waited a while before they jumped the broom. I understood why they waited so long now though, and I was in no hurry to wed, but Lord, I did want that ring. After Daddy died it took Mom a few years to date again and now she had Clarence. I called him dad too, out of respect, but he could never replace my daddy, Nathan Elton.

I got seven outfits for this weekend, and we left in the morning. He said we were going to be there in time for a good lunch and go shopping then go to the beach that night. He wanted to kiss me under the stars by the ocean. I just wanted to feel like Stella from *How Stella got her Groove Back*. Angela Bassett knew she played the hell out of that part and Taye Diggs was sexy as ever in it. I wasn't that old, but Jeremy was just as sexy as Taye. He had a six pack, nice biceps, gorgeous eyes and everything was right in place. That was my sweetheart. I loved his lips too, so juicy. I needed to stop; this weekend was not gonna be a romper room. I was determined to keep my legs closed from now on.

Who could be knocking at my door this late?

When I reached for the door, I could hear someone crying. I opened the door and Jeremy was standing there with blood all over his torn shirt. I didn't know what to think but he was not in his right mind, and I could tell by looking at him.

"Oh my God. Jeremy baby what happened?" I pulled him out of the rain. He stood there then dropped to his knees and started screaming and praying and shouting all at the same time. I stood there silently, praying and asking God to let me be able to handle whatever was going on.

He finally gained the strength to tell me what had him so upset. He went to visit Junior but when he got there, the ambulance was there, and Junior's mother was holding him. Junior had blood all over him. Jeremy said her boyfriend Mike got upset when Junior wouldn't obey his orders to turn the television and started beating him. When she finally got to Junior his body was still and he was bleeding profusely. She called the police, but Mike beat her too. The crazy fool left before the police got there. Jeremy didn't know what to do other than to let them take Junior to the hospital.

I was waiting for him to tell me the worst, but he said they got him there just in time. Two of his ribs, his nose and his left arm were broken. He also had a bad bruise on his forehead. The blood on his shirt was Junior's, not Mike's as I had suspected. There was a warrant out for his arrest, but Jeremy had hate in his eyes. I had never seen him like this, and I didn't know what to do.

I finally got him to take off his clothes and ran him a bath with lavender oil in it. I let him soak and didn't bother him for a couple of hours. When I finally peeked into the bathroom, he was asleep in the tub. I woke him up easily and got him out of the tub, dried him off then put him to bed. We didn't say a word for the rest of the night. I knew we were not going to the Bahamas any time soon.

For two days, Jeremy stayed at the hospital until they practically had to throw him out. He didn't go to work today and didn't plan on going tomorrow. I went with him Sunday after church, and it was so sad looking at Junior sitting in that bed with tubes attached to him. They said one of the broken ribs punctured his lung and he needed help breathing. The first couple of days he was in intensive care.

There had been no sign of Mike. Jamika was full of worry and regret. She was starting to seem human to me but that was to be expected. Any real mother would be concerned about her child after what Junior had been through. She even said she would sign over her parental rights because she couldn't deny that her poor choices almost cost her their child.

The surprising thing was Jeremy still wanted to go ahead with our plans to visit the Bahamas. He said we would go in three months because by then hopefully Junior would be out of the hospital and home with him. He waited until we were home from the hospital

Sunday to shout for joy about Jamika's decision. He had told her he would put her through the ringer over everything and she bowed out gracefully. She didn't want to be put through all of that after what happened. Jeremy would have been relentless, and she knew it. I couldn't do anything but praise God with him.

I was happy when he said he still wanted to go to the Bahamas. He said he would let Junior stay with his mother while we were vacationing, and he wanted to go for a full week instead of just a weekend. We were still going to therapy as well, every week like clockwork. Our therapist said our reaction to the situation with Junior was a good sign of how we would be able to handle future calamities in our lives.

All I had to say was I couldn't wait to be called Junior's mother legally. But maybe I was jumping the gun. I should get a ring and wedding first, right? I could not afford to take the attention off the direction of our relationship even if Junior was sick. I had to stay the course. It had been six months since we got back together and when we went to the Bahamas it would be nine months. That was plenty of time for him to propose. *Lord let's get there already.*

TWELVE

Mama don't stop me now

We had two months to go before this wedding but too much stuff was still up in the air. I found out Mama did not make the final payment to the reception venue and now she was nowhere to be found. I couldn't understand what she thought this was. Isaac said he knew she would pull something crazy like this to make a point. I told him not to worry about it, but it was starting to cause me too much stress.

I'd been having chest pains, but I didn't want to tell anybody. If I said something to Isaac, he was going to have a fit. I couldn't wait until I saw Delores Renee Mosley. I was going to let her have it as soon as I found her. There was no excuse for her behavior. I should have known she would try one more thing to stop this wedding.

If she had her way, we would not have anything in place. I was glad Isaac gave her a check for everything she had paid so far. She came to me and gave it back, saying that Daddy would roll over in his grave if he knew she kept it. But all that did was put her back in the driver's seat. It didn't matter though. I already knew Isaac would pay it if she refused.

Now all I had to do was try on this gown one last time. I decided to go by myself this last time because I did not want anybody else's opinions. Plus, Regina had her hands full now with helping Jeremy with Junior. I couldn't believe everything that little boy had been through. God was good; at least he didn't have any permanent injuries. When they caught that fool, I hoped they would put him under the jail.

My dress was gorgeous. The lace appliques were beautiful. I picked out my veil and looked in the mirror. Before I knew it, I was crying.

"What's the matter sweetie?" Shelly, the seamstress, asked, rubbing my shoulders.

"I wish I could have my mother here to share in this moment. She is ruining everything. I don't know what else to do." I felt defeated.

"Do you love him?"

"Yes, dearly." I wiped my tears away.

"That's all that matters. Even if nobody else shows up, as long as you and him make those vows that's all that's needed. Don't let your mother ruin your life because she can't accept him. You prayed about it and got an answer from God, right?"

"Yes. I pray every day and God told me he was the one."

"Then marry him girl and live your life for you and him and nobody else." She gave me a hug then pulled the veil over my face. I stood there and looked in the mirror at Keisha Renee Mosley. I was a woman of great beauty, and I was at peace. No matter what Mama said or did from now on, I was going to marry Isaac.

Almost a whole week passed, and my mother was still nowhere to be found. The Kelton House called and said they would not be able to hold it any longer without the final payment. My heart skipped a beat as a thought flashed through my mind. What if this was a sign, we should not get married? What if God was using my mother to stop me from making a big mistake? What if Isaac was not the one? Before I knew it, I fell off the chair and hit the ground hard. Isaac came running in the kitchen.

"Keisha, baby what's wrong?" He yelled.

"My chest." I was holding my left arm in excruciating pain. He didn't hesitate in calling the paramedics. When they came, they said I may have had a heart attack and rushed me to the hospital. Isaac got in touch with Granny Barb. She said she would have my cousin take her to the hospital.

I sat in the hospital for almost three days before my mama showed up. She tried to act like this was a sign. I let her have it. I didn't hold anything back, but my pulse started to climb. They told my mother she had to leave but not before Isaac pulled her to the side outside my room.

"Delores, I have tried to respect you, but this is going too far. If you cannot accept me as her husband, I think it would be best if you would leave us alone so we can live our lives. I love your daughter, but this medical emergency has shown to me that she is too stressed out about all this. If we have to, we will go down to the courthouse and be married with our friends there to witness it. This whole wedding was nothing more than a party that you wanted to show off in front of people who Keisha doesn't care about. I love her too much to let you ruin this. You don't have to make the last payment to the Kelton House. Just leave us alone." He walked back into my room and closed the door behind him not letting her say a word.

The next day I got an email from the Kelton House saying the final payment had been made. I didn't want to, but I called my mother anyway.

"Mama, I got an email that they received the final payment for the venue. What happened?"

"I paid for it. Your fiancé finally stood up and proved to me how much he really loved you. Him telling me that I had to choose to be out of your life or get with the program was too much for me to bear. Your father would have a fit when I got to heaven. I love you Keisha and I want you to be happy. If Isaac is the man you want, so be it. I will not stand in the way anymore. You got about six weeks left so what else do we need to do?"

I sat there staring at the phone in disbelief for almost three minutes until I heard her yelling my name. I snapped out of it and told her we just had to make all the rest of the final payments to the caterer and florist.

Mama was finally fully on board. I was so excited I told her to come over on Sunday after church so she could see my dress. She said she couldn't wait to see it. I did tell her that it was my final choice and all the alterations had already been done so she couldn't make any changes. She agreed and we said, "I love you," then hung up.

I wiggled a jig really quick then went to hug my soon-to-be husband. He was happy Mama chose to stay in our lives. It wouldn't have been the same without her. We weren't allowed to have any frolicking for about another week, so we made out like we were teenagers that night.

We did our final walk through of the Kelton House then contacted the caterer to set up our final tasting. I couldn't believe it. I was going to marry Isaac and my mother was not going to stop me.

THIRTEEN

I'll pass

Our wedding was to die for. My mother gave us a toast that was not too out of line. She danced with Isaac and gave us a nice monetary gift that she said Daddy kept tucked away especially for this occasion. I was sitting there taking it all in looking out at the ocean in Cozumel with Isaac laying in my lap. I couldn't believe I was finally married. After all the turmoil we had been through with my mother, we made it down the aisle and now we had forever to love one another.

Today was our last day here and we would be on the plane going home in about five hours. I hated to move him but had to get packed up. He had stuff thrown all over the place. On our first day at Cozumel Palace, we didn't leave the room. He made sure we weren't disturbed, and I found out the hard way he was a beast in the bedroom. We had committed to not having sex the last month before our wedding so it would seem new to us, and boy, was it ever.

The next day when we finally came out of our trance, we went to breakfast in the hotel's restaurant, the Turquesa. Then we headed over to the beach to take in some sun. I got to shop a bit the other day and we did a lot of sight-seeing and a little snorkeling. We had so much fun and made a promise that for our ten-year anniversary we would return. The beaches were beautiful, and the people were interesting to say the least. Though I generally didn't like Mexican food, I fell in love with their savory dishes and margaritas.

Overall, it was a wonderful honeymoon. We got a call from his ex-wife two days ago but ignored it. I didn't have time for that trollop trying to mess up anything. She refused to allow the kids to come to the wedding even after he said he would sue her for joint custody. I didn't know why Loretta was hell-bent on trying to make our day miserable. He was upset about it but got over it when he received a phone call from his daughter who sang him his favorite song before the ceremony began. Angela was such a little darling. She could do no wrong in his eyes. She was a Daddy's girl. Little Isaac was a mess though, but he loved him just the same.

I couldn't wait to get back home and start the process of changing my name. I ordered thank you cards and monogrammed towel sets while we were here. I called Regina to see what she was up to. She asked why I was calling her. Had the nerve to say not to worry about her; worry about pleasing my husband while we were in paradise. I hoped one day I could give her the same advice.

Mama called three days after we got here. Isaac answered the phone by calling her mom. She didn't correct him which showed much promise. She said she wanted to make sure we were still breathing. I knew she just missed my voice. We talked on the phone every day since I left for college years ago. She would always be my number one, though I was married now. I didn't want her to ever feel left out. She was going to need us in her later years.

When we got back home there was so much mail and gifts that Mama had I could hardly keep up with it. I was still beaming. I'd never felt a love like this before. I sometimes found myself looking at him in total disbelief. Even when he farted, I giggled. It was like I found something new all over again.

Married life was going to be good. I could tell that already. We got into a little tiff at the airport on the way home when they couldn't find our bags. But we made up before we got on the shuttle to our car. His best friend Marcus, who was the best man, sent us a two-hundred-dollar gift card to my favorite store Target. In the card he wrote, *don't spend it all at once, Kiesha.* He was a knucklehead.

It had been three days since we got back. Now I am waiting for Sears to deliver my new washer and dryer. That was my wedding gift. I got a top of line Whirlpool set with every feature you could imagine.

"Hello?" I opened the door to find a police officer standing there.

"Hello, Ma'am. I'm looking for an Isaac Antonio Lampley."

"That's my husband." I said, shocked. I couldn't imagine what he wanted with my babe.

"Is he here, Mrs. Lampley?" he asked, pretty much dismissing my presence. There was another officer in the squad car.

"What do you want with him?" I asked, not falling for the okie doke.

"If you would just tell him to come to door, Ma'am. I have a warrant for his arrest." He pulled out a piece of paper and handed it to me. I shouted for my husband and read the letter. When he came downstairs, the police officer barged into our house.

"Wait, wait a minute you just can't barge in here, sir." I said, trying to get between them.

"What in the world is going on?" Isaac stood there in his boxers, totally unaware of what was going on.

"Isaac Antonio Lampley, you are under arrest," the police officer said, and started reading him his rights. He wasn't going to let him put any clothes on until I started acting like a fool. I threw myself onto my husband and begged him to give him some dignity. The police officer allowed him ten minutes to get dressed. We went upstairs and I showed him the warrant.

After reading it then re-reading it, he instructed me to call his lawyer. He went downstairs with his shoulders slumped, trying to keep his head up. I could tell he was torn apart by this. I couldn't believe he was being charged with child molestation from his own daughter. I knew it was a lie from the pits of hell. *Devil, I don't care what you throw at us; we are going to pass this test.* Loretta set this up just to wreak havoc in our lives. God was still in control no matter what. I didn't have any doubt.

FOURTEEN

You gotta let God do it

It had been several days since Isaac came home from jail. It only took a couple of hours to get him out, but of course, when we got home, Loretta started in on him. That woman had the nerve to come to our home and threaten to tear us apart for what allegedly happened to Angela. The funny thing about it all was that she was so determined to kill his spirit she let it slip that she told Angela how to answer the questions from the psychologist.

Right then I knew this was a deliberate stunt by her to ruin us. He was not allowed to see his children while under investigation. He was so sick about it he stayed in bed for three days. I had to plow him out. The room was starting to permeate with a funk I had never smelled before. He was a broken man. He refused to eat or go to work. Finally, I had enough and lost it.

I couldn't tell my friends or my mother about any of this. They would never understand. Loretta said she was going to make sure the entire world knew he was a pervert. But I had suspicions that the witch's new boyfriend did it. All of a sudden, she had a new man who none of us ever heard her talking about, but she claimed he had been around for years. In order for her to keep screwing him, she wanted to mess up a good man's life and ruin her child's future. She was disgusting and I hated her. If I could go to her job and whoop her tail.

I was disappointed in my husband too. His reaction should have been one of anger but instead he'd been sulking and depressed. He hadn't mentioned he was innocent, which made me wonder a little. But I knew he was innocent. I didn't care what Loretta said, that man would never hurt his own flesh and blood. I would fight for us if he wouldn't. The devil was a liar. I needed to talk to someone about all this. My life had been turned upside down because of this madness. I was going to call Regina. She would be understanding. She'd gone through something similar with her man's child. I was hesitant to call but I had the phone against my ear expecting her answering it.

"Hey girlie, I haven't heard from you since the wedding. How's married life?"

I broke down. I was crying so much my eyes were bulging. She hung up the phone and within fifteen minutes there was a frantic knock at the door. My best friend was standing there in the rain with her hair pulled back and what looked like to be some Vaseline on her face.

I started laughing.

"This ain't funny. I thought somebody was beating on you or something. I came rushing over here ready to Kirk out on somebody."

"Good, keep that spirit up because after I tell you what happened you're going to want to beat somebody's tail." I let her in. We hugged then I sat down. She followed my cue and didn't say a word, just listened. I poured out my heart to her and told her everything that had happened since we got home from our honeymoon. It had been less than a month and my world was now full of chaos.

"So how are you doing in all of this?" she asked.

"As well as to be expected. Today was the first day I cried about it. I wasn't going to say anything to anybody," I admitted.

"Girl why? We both know this is a lie straight from the pits of hell. Don't you believe him? He did say he didn't do it... right?"

"I was going to get to that. He hasn't officially said he was innocent. He's just been moping around in a daze. I know his work is being affected because his boss called me and asked if he was okay. He was at work and broke down crying in his office at a meeting. That's not like him at all. He is usually so strong."

"He's still in shock. Isaac is a simple man; he doesn't know how to react to something so devilish."

"I know. But we got to get started on defending him. His lawyer has called every day, but Isaac won't speak with him. I don't know what to do. I want to call his mother, but I don't want him to get mad at me for telling anybody. Please don't say anything. If Loretta had her way, the news people would be all over this but he's not a high-profile person in the city. I can't believe all of this is happening." I began crying again. Regina sat there and let me cry. She knew I needed to get it out. Then she got up and made us some herbal tea.

We strategized on how I could get Isaac to show signs of life. How I could get him to talk about it and admit the truth, whatever that may be? I was going to stand by my husband. I already knew none of these accusations were true, but the police had to have some kind of evidence to arrest him. I didn't know what that could be though.

It had been a week, and he was still barely talking. I'd had enough. Today he was going to tell me what was going on. I made his favorite meal, fried chicken, collard greens, sweet potatoes and homemade cornbread. He would be home in less than fifteen minutes. I cleaned up everything and put his favorite channel on the TV so he could look at Sports Center while I finished the cornbread.

Regina said to talk slow and be optimistic. Show him that I was on his side no matter what he confessed to. I couldn't imagine that any of this would be true. Isaac didn't have it in him to do anything so gross. Still though, there was a reason he was refusing to deal with it. I just hoped I could stick to my word and stand by him no matter what. In good times and bad, that was what the preacher said. He was coming through the garage door.

"Hello handsome," I said as he stood there in one of his many pinstriped blue Macy's suits.

"Hello sweetie. Is that what I think it is?" He walked past me and straight to the stove. He started to loosen his tie and unbutton his top two buttons on his shirt. Then he put his finger in the sweet potatoes, and I popped him.

"Wash your hands!" I demanded. He turned and smiled a weak smile like he was still feeling defeated. The spark in his eyes was gone. They looked dark and hollow. He had bags underneath each eye that seemed to develop overnight. "Let me make our plates; unless you want to sit and watch Sports Center for a sec?"

"Naw, I'll be right back down. You're looking good by the way; I like the bangs." He walked toward the stairs. I changed my hair almost three days ago. I thought he hadn't noticed. When he came back downstairs, he had on his Cavaliers jersey with matching shorts. He loved Lebron James though he was no longer apart of the team. We sat and ate silently at the dining room table. Finally, I broke in with, "So when do you want to talk about the elephant in the room?"

"What's that?"

"Isaac don't do that. You know we haven't discussed these trumped up charges against you. We both know it's a lie and Loretta is just trying to cause chaos in your new life."

"Yeah, I know that. I didn't think I had to tell you that I didn't do it. I would never intentionally hurt my flesh and blood. Angela is my angel, which is why I named her Angela. I thought I couldn't have kids, but she was born first. I would do anything for her. I don't know what could be going on in Loretta's mind to make her do this."

"The lawyer said you may have to go to trial about this unless the charges get dropped by some miracle. How are we going to pay for any of this?"

"You're worried about paying for it and I'm worried about my daughter's safety. You do know something had to happen for this to go this far, which means she is in danger, and she doesn't feel safe enough to tell me, her own father, the truth."

"How do you know she is in danger?"

"She mentioned that things were changing at home a couple of days before we got married. She wanted to move here with us. Then her mother grabbed the phone and hit her while I listened to her chastise her over the phone. She didn't know she was talking to me though because I heard her begging her to tell her who she was telling their business to. I guess Loretta feels like if she could blame me for this, she doesn't have to worry about me coming after her for custody and she can break us up at the same time. But you know what? God is good and faithful to those who are faithful to him. I'm going to pass this test and we are all going to be fine. I'm not hungry right now; I'll be back." He got up from the table and leaned in to kiss me on the forehead. "Don't worry your pretty little head, this will all be over sooner than you think." He put his plate in the microwave, got his jacket, opened the garage door and left in his car. He had a look in his eye that was familiar again, the look of determination. He was starting to fight for his life, our life and the lives of his children.

I finished eating by my lonesome and then cleaned the kitchen. It seemed like hours had gone by when I heard the garage door open. My husband walked back into the house with a box of files. He had been to the OSU law library researching the case and custody procedures. He was not going out without a fight and needed to be prepared for anything the devil was going to throw at him. He was sure that if he let God do it, everything was going to work out in our favor.

The past two weeks had been horrible. First they made discovery; they found Angela's underwear from the night she was molested. But we got a break; the semen sample did not match Isaac or any man in her family line for that matter. So of course, they dropped the charges and started looking at Loretta's new live-in boyfriend. Come to find out the man had a past of hurting little girls. He was a registered sex offender in Georgia and his paperwork got misplaced when he moved to Ohio, which was why he was under the radar.

The look on that tramp's face when that came out was priceless. But of course, it couldn't be that simple. She wouldn't press any charges, but since she and Isaac had joint custody, he did it for her ignorant tail. The tramp had the nerve to hit him in front of the police and he had her arrested. Then the kids had to come and stay with us.

And staying with us was something I wasn't ready for, to say the least. It never crossed my mind that we would end up with full custody of two pre-teens. Angela was twelve and Isaac was eleven. They were a handful.

I couldn't believe how much like his daddy the little boy was until he tore up my bathroom the first night he was there. I couldn't tell if someone had died in there or he did the number two. Angela was another story all together. She barely let anyone touch her stuff and she was exceptionally clean. She took four showers the first day she was here. I let her do that for about three days when finally, I told her she could only shower one time in the morning and one time before bed. At first, she scoffed at me then she fell in line after her dad talked to her.

He said she told him she felt like she was dirty. She didn't like the way boys looked at her now. At only twelve, she looked sixteen, shapely in all the right places. I knew the little boys would be on her. One of the little buzzards tried to touch her butt on the playground and she beat the boy down like he stole something.

Isaac was worried she was changing for the worse. I didn't want to agree with him, but she was becoming more defiant. Motherhood was not going too good for me as their stepmom. But I had to get it together. He was hell bent on gaining full custody and Loretta still hadn't made bail. I had to let God take control in this whole situation. This was my life now regardless of whether I was ready for it.

FIFTEEN

What is Divine?

We'd been going strong and today we had another session with our counselor. She said we had two more sessions left unless we wanted to continue for the rest of the year. I thought we needed a little more help, but he thought we'd be okay without it. Today she said we were going to deal with what she saw as the major dilemma in our relationship.

I couldn't imagine it could be anything other than trusting one another enough to let everything come out in the open. When he refused to tell me about Junior for all those years it hurt me. I didn't believe he was in love with me, or he would have been open enough to tell me the truth years ago. Now he was like a faucet, telling me every little thing that he thought would be important.

We were meeting to get a late lunch at the Cheesecake Factory first. Our counselor was at Easton, so it would be easy to get there on time. I loved the chicken littles dish they served, and he liked the roasted corn. As we made it over to the counselor's office, we held hands and daydreamed aloud about how our life was going to be in the future.

When we got to the doctor's office all bets were off. She had a scowl on her face and looked like she was ready for war. She started off asking us about what Jeremy meant by his statement that our love was so divine that even the devil couldn't touch it. At first, I laughed it off, but she was serious.

"You do know what you professed was close to blasphemy. How can you have divine love with a human, and you are not God? You can't possibly give anyone divine love," Dr. Mars said.

"But our love is divinely ordained by God. He put us together and he has kept us together," Jeremy tried to explain.

"No that is not what you meant, and I knew it by what you said. You said your love was divine, not ordained, which is something entirely different. Minister Spencer, you should know better and when I realized you were committing a horrible sin by professing those words, I didn't know how to react. The essence of divinity is God. I know you both know this, right?"

"I mean yeah, but I think what he meant was our love is divinely ordained because it was sent by God."

"Oh really? Then every relationship is divinely ordained whether you believe in God or not, correct? Because you don't have to know or believe in God to be in a relationship, right? God does not have to be the center of every relationship, nor is he ever really. Most relationships come out of convenience which is what I think Jeremy has found and the reason why he selfishly compared the love he has for you with the love God has for you. He wants to be the demigod in your life because he thinks you can't do any better. He doesn't feel he can either. Which is okay if you want to settle. But be honest about it; don't try to make it something, it is not just because you are too afraid to go after what you really want. And if you really want each other, then be satisfied in that but don't mock God doing it. I think you both need to repent for being selfish and prideful," Dr. Mars said, and then started writing in her notepad.

I felt like I had just been hit by a Mack truck. How dare she, but how dare he? I never thought about it that way, but I could tell by how he reacted that she was right. He sat there and fidgeted, then put his head down when she said he was settling.

"Is this true? Are you just settling for me Jeremy? Was there someone else and it didn't work out? Please tell me the truth. I can take the truth, but I will not live a lie." I begged him to answer me. He sat there with the dumbest look on his face then he spoke.

"There was a woman named Katlynn I did fall in love with. But she married someone else two years ago. Since then, I have been pining away trying to make sense of it all and what she told me days before she left. She told me I always compared everyone I dated to you. She said I should stop being a fool and go after what my heart wanted, and God had already given me. She said I should tell you the truth about Junior and let the chips fall where they may. I didn't want to believe her but then I looked at all my past relationships since you. None of them ever turned into anything and each of them said I was not vested in a future with them or that something was holding me back. It was you. It always has been you. I made a mistake with my baby mama, and I didn't know how I was ever going to make that up to you."

Tears were rolling down his face as he finally told me what happened the weekend, he slept with her. I didn't know she was a one-night stand. I always assumed they had a relationship. He said he wanted to wait to be with me, but he couldn't bear the teasing from his friends and thought she would go away without ever having to deal with her again. When he found out she was pregnant, he panicked, and that was how our relationship turned sour. He always sat in church, staring at me from the pulpit and fantasizing about marrying me and having a family. When he finally finished, I felt liberated. Dr. Mars said she understood now why he felt that our love was divine, but we still needed to pray and repent and get forgiveness from God and each other. I was determined to be the help meet he would need for the rest of his life.

A couple of weeks after our last counseling session, Jeremy and I went to see his mother. She was pleasantly surprised to see me. Mrs. Spencer or Mama Cicely was a gem. She always hugged me at church and kept trying to get us to come over for dinner. I didn't know why he never took me over here, but she was excited to see me.

When we got there, there was stuff everywhere. It looked like her place had been through a hurricane. Jeremy smiled and acted like everything was okay. She had stacks of newspapers behind the door, three couches in the living room and I counted five televisions. Now

I could see why he never wanted me to come over here. She was a hoarder.

The funny thing was, she was always so put together at church. That was why people had to stop looking outside all the time at what people were wearing to church. Too many people were hurting on the inside, and we were so caught up in the new Rolex we saw them wearing that we forget to ask them how they were feeling. I didn't know what could be done to help Mama Cicely, but I knew I had to do something.

"You look beautiful," she said while trying to tug at my hair. I let her do it and tried not to show the disdain I had for her now. The house smelled awful. I knew if I opened the refrigerator something dead would be in there. Jeremy walked on through the maze of confusion and went upstairs.

Mama Cicely made a space on the couch for me to sit down. I was apprehensive but I didn't want to offend her, so I sat but kept my purse on my lap. She could tell I was uncomfortable.

"I know it looks bad chile, but I just don't want to let some things go, that's all. Jeremy has been helping me though, it used to be much worse." Saying that showed promise; she knew she had a problem, which meant she could change. Jeremy came back downstairs and pulled out a chair. We then started a conversation like nothing was in disarray. He invited her to dinner with us, but she declined, saying that she had cooked something. I hoped like hell she didn't ask us if we wanted a taste.

We went to dinner at P.F. Chang's in Easton. He told me more about his mother. She had a nervous breakdown six years ago after his father died. Mr. Spencer died suddenly in his sleep while they were in the bed together. She always blamed herself and said that he would haunt her for the rest of her days. Jeremy couldn't get her to realize he had just had a heart attack which was expected with the way he lived.

Ever since then she had been holding on to things left and right. She read the newspaper every day and kept them in the living room so she could remember what happened the days before she decided to leave her house. He said it was her prison and he wished he could get her out of there. After she had the nervous breakdown, a therapist came to the house and that was when things started to get better.

Now he came over two days a week and threw stuff away that he knew she hadn't seen in over three years. He started upstairs in his bedroom so she wouldn't notice too much but he couldn't get rid of things that he knew she held onto from his past. I said a silent prayer about the whole thing while he explained it to me. I hoped he wouldn't take on all her baggage now, even though I knew in my heart he would. He had Junior and Mama Cicely pulling him at every angle; I didn't know if I would be able to fit in anywhere. But I was determined to be there for him and his family.

SIXTEEN

A wish come true

It seemed as soon as we asked for forgiveness the cloud of oppression lifted off our lives and our relationship. Jeremy started to open up more. He was full of promise when it came to the future of our relationship. I got a raise on my job and an opportunity to work as a teacher for the Ohio State University Young Scholars summer institute. I was geeked. Even Lil Jeremy was thinking of engaging with his mother.

He vowed that he didn't want to see her again when he got out of the hospital. I had to pray every night for weeks that their situation turned around. She almost got the boy killed but she was still his mother, and that relationship was going to be vital to all his other relationships with women in the future. He asked me if I would be his mommy. I cried at the thought of it all.

Jeremy went and put the wheels in motion for me to adopt him the next day. He said he couldn't believe he was going to get everything he had been praying for since we met. His mother was cleaning the house on her own too. Now that everything was falling into place, I knew he would propose soon. We were on our way to the movies when I brought up the subject again.

"Since you've started talking to the lawyers about adoption when are we going to make this official?"

"We are official," he said, oblivious to what I was really asking.

"Jeremy, you can't be that blind. I want to get married."

"What size ring do you wear again?"

"I've told you three times already. Why are you stalling? Everything else is falling into place. What in the world is holding you back?"

"Nothing. I just haven't gotten the ring yet and I want to go to the Bahamas and do it up like I always wanted to."

"I couldn't care less about all of that. You know what, never mind. I'm not going through any adoption procedures until we've been married for at least three years. Therefore, you don't need to meet with the lawyers anymore about that. I don't think you're serious, so let's just enjoy our friendship and let everything else just go. I don't feel like going to the movies so can you please take me home now?"

"Where is all of this coming from?" His voice cracked.

"You can't be serious. How long have we been dating each other off and on, ten years?" I asked.

"Roughly ten years. But we've been apart for most of that time. I want to marry you Regina, but I don't want to do it half way. You deserve the best. I know you want a big wedding, even bigger than Keisha's. I've been saving for a couple of months now and have a ring in sight. Don't worry, we will get there, I promise. Do you really want to go home for real?"

"Yes, take me home." We drove in silence as he drove on 270 to the east side of Columbus. When we got in front of my house, I was about to open the door when he said, "What if we eloped?"

"What!" I couldn't believe my ears.

"Yeah, I have enough for the ring and maybe a weekend in Vegas. We could do it there and then come home and get everything in order for the adoption. You could move into my house, and we could sell yours, or better yet rent it out and make some money. What do you say?"

"Boy, you haven't even asked me to marry you officially yet. No, I don't want to run off and get married like that. It feels cheap and forced. But you have until the end of this month to ask or keep it moving."

He leaned over and kissed me.

"Or keep it moving?" We gazed at each other as my heart rushed. He put his hand in my hair then kissed me again and we started making out like teenagers. He asked could he come inside. I told him no, even though I could see he was more than ready to make me climb the walls. My hair was all over my head, but I got out of the car and tried to walk to the house with a little dignity.

"Are you sure?" he yelled from the car. I waved him off and got my butt in the house. He texted me that he loved me, and I texted back.

I knew he would ask me, but he was taking entirely too long. But at least he was taking all the steps to make us a family.

It was August 30, and I was on pins and needles. I had given Jeremy an ultimatum three weeks ago. He hadn't been as talkative as he used to be and sometimes, I felt like I did the wrong thing. We were going to dinner at the Ocean Club at Easton. I decided to dress up a bit and show off my assets. Even though I wasn't a ten, I could be a solid eight with my thick legs and shapely thighs. I used to get teased about it when I was in high school but when I got to college, the boys saw it as my best feature.

When he finally showed up, he looked a little unsure of himself. He kissed me on the forehead then put me in the car. We barely spoke until his phone rang. It was Junior; I could hear his squeaky voice asking him if he was ready. I broke out into a wide grin and relaxed.

As we sat down at our table, people were looking at us, and one lady asked how long we had been married? She was with her husband who looked like he was a kid in the candy store. Jeremy said we weren't married yet, but he was changing that as soon as possible. He ordered some white wine then this guy came to our table and started to serenade me with Brian McKnight's, "Love of my Life". I sat there blushing with tears running down my face. Jeremy came and kneeled on my right side and then he finally asked me.

Regina, we have been the best of friends for many years. But you are not just a friend to me. You are my lover, my confidant, and the woman who I want to spend the rest of my life with. Will you please marry me?" I looked at him and then the guy whose wife asked if we were married said,

"Gone girl and marry that man." I laughed and finally answered.

"Yes, Jeremy Marquis Spencer, I will marry you." He jumped up and pulled me to him. Then he picked me up and shouted across the room.

"She said yes!" He was so happy, and I was overjoyed. We ate our dinner in haste and then we left to go to my parent's house. Mama and Daddy were sitting in the living room as usual watching re-runs of *Law and Order*. She saw the goofy look on our faces and laughed.

"So, you finally asked my daughter to marry you," Mama said while knitting what looked to be a handkerchief. Daddy looked at us and started laughing too.

"Bernice, I think they might make it. It took him ten years, three break ups, a baby and finally an ultimatum to finally make my daughter happy." He was being sarcastic, but it did sting a little. Jeremy sat next to daddy and apologized. Apparently, he had been over there earlier and asked them for my hand in marriage. I had no clue. Mama baked us a carrot cake, our favorite, so we went into the kitchen and prepared plates for our men.

"Don't let what your father said get to you. Ten years is a long time, but he made the necessary adjustments to make you, his wife. He told us today he was scared of not being who you really wanted. I had to tell the boy the truth. You had never gotten over him and would probably never let him go in your heart. He said he didn't know that but now he understood why your friendship lasted for so long. I love him like my son already. But you gotta start standing up for yourself. No more waiting to be fed, take the initiative and go after what you want from him. Be up front and direct in the beginning of the marriage so you can never say your needs aren't being met. Take it from me; it works wonders for your marriage's survival. I'm proud of you baby." She hugged me and started to cry.

"Let me look at that ring on your finger. He showed it to us earlier. I bet he paid a nice piece of change for it." We giggled and fussed over the ring then brought the cake and tea to the men. We had some good laughs over our past ten years as we reminisced with my parents. Then we went and told his mother. She had the whole living room clear of clutter. She shouted for joy and did a quick jig. I let her serve us some coffee from that dirty kitchen, but I prayed really good over it first.

SEVENTEEN

The next time I will know

I was getting impatient with the police because for some reason the case against my husband was still open. He was going to be exonerated from all the charges but for some reason they wanted to keep pestering us. Finally, I had one of my Sorors, who was a judge, call the detective in charge and find out what the hell was the hold up. After that he was officially exonerated, and everything was put to rest.

They were now looking at Loretta's live-in boyfriend. They had a good case against him and were ready to make a formal arrest. Then that crazy heffa decided to come home and try and get the kids back. Why in the world did she do that crap? She had only been out of jail for two days but apparently, she did not take any of that time to wise up. Isaac had them serve her with papers to get full custody. She had a conniption. The fool came to our house with a bunch of suitcases, screaming and hollering for us to open the door. Isaac let her make a scene because he had called the police as soon as her car showed up in front of the house. Angela and little Isaac were crying and screaming too. I couldn't believe I was in the middle of this circus.

When the police came, she reluctantly left the premises. The officer asked Isaac if he wanted to file a report and he said yes but did not go downtown to ask for a restraining order. He said she had one more time to act a fool and he was going to make sure she would never see the kids again. I didn't want to hear him say that, but Loretta had gone too far.

Now he was full of anger and resentment. He hated her. I couldn't help but pray for her and the entire situation. I didn't know if I could take anymore craziness.

We took the kids to the zoo the next weekend.

While we were there, Angela shared with me that she liked a boy at school. He was new to the city and didn't know anything about what had happened to her. Though they had moved away from their mother's house, some little girl who was her arch enemy started telling her business all in the streets. For her to only be twelve years old, she had forty-year-old woman problems.

I felt like I was out of control of the situation. I couldn't do anything but pray every night and be an open ear for both. Warming up to them was becoming easier and I had created a planned weekly agenda that kept the house running smoothly. Mama called almost every night to see how everything was going.

She was deeply concerned. She knew I had not spent much time with his kids since we started dating and especially after we got engaged. Mama was cool about it though. She took them on a shopping spree right before they went back to school.

For the most part, everything was coming together. I decided to go over to visit with Mama for a few hours after work today mainly because I needed a break from home. But I was totally unprepared for what I was about to find out.

Mama was on the phone when I walked through the back door, and she had the speaker phone on in the kitchen. I didn't pay it no mind until I heard her old friend ask her how the chemo was going. Mama said it was going all right and that the doctors were optimistic. I was floored.

"Mama what are you talking about. Do you have cancer?"

"Jazzy, I'll call you back." She stood there looking like she had just got caught with her pants down. "Baby girl, we need to talk."

"It's a yes or no answer."

"Yes." Her head dropped.

"How could you keep something like this from me? I'm gonna lose you too? Just like I lost daddy. How could you do this to me?" I started to yell at her, then like a spoiled brat, I began stomping my feet and waving my arms in the air. She tried to console me.

"No! No! How could you, Mama?" Tears were rolling down my face. I was so hurt.

"Baby girl, I didn't know how to tell you. You were so happy with everything else that was going on in your life I didn't want to bring you down with my bad news. But it's going to be okay. I promise." She reached to try and pinch my cheek like she used to do when I was a little girl.

"That's the same thing Daddy said, remember? Then he died." I stormed out of the house. I didn't know where I was going but I was done. I couldn't take it anymore. First my husband's mess with his daughter and now this. God had a lot of explaining to do. How did he expect me to get through all of this on my own? I couldn't imagine looking at my mother in a hospital bed. But I knew it was coming.

God always answered prayers, even if they were not the answers we wanted. Right now, I just want my mother to be healed. I pulled the car over in the parking lot at Polaris Mall and began to weep. I was weeping like I never had before. So many things were going wrong, and it hadn't been three months since I got married. Was this the life I had to look forward to? *Lord, I thought you said your love was divine. This doesn't feel like you love me at all.*

EIGHTEEN

You better know who I am

Keisha

I couldn't believe my mother had breast cancer. She'd known about it for over a year but never told anybody in the family. She said the only one who knew was her best friend. I was her best friend. She should have told me. I would've been able to understand why she was acting so crazy for all those months.

I told Isaac and he said he would go and talk to her. I didn't want her to be upset with me for telling him. He said he was going tonight after work. He'd better be on the up and up though, because Delores still hadn't totally accepted him in the family even though we were married. I didn't want this all to backfire.

He said he had to pray for a major decision after finding out about this. After trying to press him to tell me, he closed the discussion and said to pray for him and my mother. But I had been praying. How do you keep praying when it seems like God isn't listening to you? So much was going on right now.

Life could not get any worse. I didn't know what else to do. Regina and I had been through the fire this year even though this was supposed to be the best year for me as a newlywed. She finally got that man to settle down and I knew he was going to pop the question any day now. We should be in bliss right now.

After they caught Isaac wife's boyfriend in Akron, he plead guilty and that should have been the end of it as far as the law went. Cleaning up the bigger issue, that poor child's self-esteem, was going to take years. She was refusing to talk about it and now she'd been asking to wear makeup. I didn't think she should yet but the girls in her class had already started.

I told her she could wear lip gloss only. Why did I do that, Jesus? She came back in the house with the loudest red color she could find, and it was the luscious kind so her lips were super juicy. She looked like a tramp. But I could never say that out loud. Lord, I didn't know how to be a mother to a little girl.

It seemed like I couldn't even figure out how to be a good wife either because we hadn't had sex since we got back from the honeymoon. It had been almost three months already, but I dared not say anything because he was going through so much with the kids. I felt awkward trying to get it started with the kids in the house.

My husband came home.

"Hello sweetie, how did everything go?" I asked.

"First things first, come here and give me some sugar." He pulled me to him without taking off his coat. He planted a kiss on me that made my toes tickle.

"Wow, what has gotten into you?" I asked when we finally came up for air. He took off his coat and smiled. Then he blew my mind.

"I'm going to have the vasectomy reversed. I talked to Mama and told her I would do anything to help her get through this. She said she wanted a grandbaby of her own. I told her about the procedure. She got upset at first until I explained to her that it wasn't the irreversible kind. We prayed together and I made my final decision. That's what I had been praying about for a while now. I felt so bad about not telling you in the beginning then seeing you with the kids woke something up inside of me. Do you still want to have kids?"

"Are you kidding me? Of course, I do!" I screamed and we hugged and kissed some more. "Are the kids home?"

"No, they are over at a neighbors' playing."

"Good, let's get started on Lil Lampley number three." He pulled me to him then threw me over his shoulder like a cave man and ran up the stairs with me. My shoes fell off, but we made it in one piece. The sex was explosive, and I cooed in delight until we heard the kids coming in the house. He didn't want to stop so we kept going.

We had already locked the door but that didn't help because they started knocking ten minutes after calling our names from the kitchen. We started giggling and tried to ignore them until they started messing with the lock. Finally, Isaac said,

"Get away from the door, boy! This is grown folks time. Y'all go downstairs in the basement and make some hot pockets until we come out and give y'all some dinner." I could hear them whispering then Angela started giggling.

"Okay daddy. But don't make no more boys, they stink." We looked at each other laughed and continued our lovemaking for another half hour.

After Keisha told me about her mother, I couldn't stop crying. I remembered when mama was diagnosed and everything that she had to go through to survive and finally heal. The chemo, the diets, the drugs, the vomiting, and hair loss. She was in agony, but God saw fit that she was healed after fighting for four years.

I was happy for Keisha when she said Isaac decided to reverse his vasectomy so that they could have kids. She admitted that they hadn't been intimate since the honeymoon but now they were acting like dogs in heat. They snuck off when the kids were in the house and got it in. I thought that was loving of him to want to do that for her mother. Now hopefully they would have a boy and she could stop worrying about it.

Jeremy and I were going strong too. He made the travel plans for us to go to the Bahamas next month. It was going to be nice because it was cold here in Columbus. I liked late fall, but I was not looking forward to snowing in the winter. Columbus had more rain than snow in the winter anyway because it was in a valley. But when we did get snow, we really got plowed in.

Junior had decided to start visiting his mother again. It was awkward at first because he didn't want to be alone with her again, so we stayed with him. She tried to object but didn't have a foot to stand on about the issue. The custody agreement forbade her from being alone with him for more than four hours anyway, so she needed to be glad the boy even wanted to spend more than an hour with her.

I couldn't stand that woman. She always tried to make waves when there was no reason to. About four weeks after Junior got out of the hospital she showed up at his school while I was picking him up.

"What in the hell are you doing here? That's my son, not yours!" she yelled.

"I know that, but you are not allowed to be alone with him, and today is not your day to see him anyway."

"Let me find out your barren ass is trying to be a mother to my child."

"I'd be more of a mother than you were. You almost got him killed over a man, remember?"

"He's, my child!"

"You stupid fool. Either go home and let him heal in peace or I'm calling the police."

"You better not call the damn police. That's alright, I got something for your ass. You ain't marrying Jeremy. He don't want no woman who can't give him no more babies."

"That's not what he says. It's none of your business anyway. Go home, you smell like a liquor cabinet and funky booty."

She left, cursing my name and swearing she was going to get back at me. Right after she pulled off, the school bell rang. I got Junior and took him home. Since then, I'd been dedicated to being more involved in his life.

Junior said he wanted me to be his mama. I cried like a baby that day. Even though she was right, I couldn't conceive, I would love to adopt Junior. But I needed to be his father's wife before anything like that happened.

Father, I know that you are El Shedi, the great I am, and I know the power in the name of Jesus. I need you to show up in our lives. Show up and let us know again just who you are. I am expecting a miracle.

CHAPTER NINETEEN

Love won't wait.

Regina

We'd been in Nassau Bahamas for almost four days. Tomorrow was our last day and this man had not proposed yet. I was sitting on the beach by my lonesome tonight because I was so frustrated. I knew the reason he wanted to come here was so he could propose, but he wasn't showing any signs of doing anything close to that. Maybe I was wrong about him all along. Today we went shopping and he bought me some jewelry and a couple of outfits. I didn't care anything about that. Where was my doggone ring and proposal? He needed to get it together. He kept acting funny like he knew what he was supposed to do but was too scared to do it. Yesterday we were at the perfect spot, underneath a waterfall, but he fumbled around like he didn't know what he wanted to do. I didn't want to go back to our room now, but it was getting late, and I knew he was worried already.

The island was beautiful at night. You could hear some of the strangest sounds against the backdrop of the ocean waves coming ashore. I wished I could stay here to live forever. I would definitely be back one day. I would probably be by myself because he didn't seem to want to make this official. I hoped he was asleep when I got there.

"Where have you been? I just left the hotel's security team. They were about to start a search for you. You had me worried sick. It's almost two in the morning!" He yelled, but then he came and hugged me like he hadn't hugged anyone in all his life.

"I went for a walk on the beach. I'm fine." I tried not to show any emotion.

I sat on the bed, and he came and got on his knees between my legs.

"You're upset with me, aren't you?" His eyes were full of tears. My tears started to stream too.

"I don't know what you're waiting for. Why…"

He put his finger to my lips and pulled out a ring box before I could ask him why he didn't want to marry me. Before I knew it, he was asking me, and it was all a blur. It wasn't rushed but I could tell he had been practicing what he was going to say for days. Of course, I said yes, but it was our last day there now. We laid in the bed wide awake and daydreamed about our wedding for the rest of the night.

In the morning we went to breakfast on the beach, and he spilled the beans that he had planned on asking me the day we were at the waterfall. I knew that was the plan, so I asked him why he didn't do it.

"I got scared again. I didn't think it was the right timing. It wasn't natural. What I did last night felt natural even though we were both emotional. I wanted you to have a good memory of how I proposed and thought the waterfall would be the best time to do it but when I saw how anxious you were I chickened out. I'm sorry babe." I smacked him gently on his forehead then kissed him.

"It really didn't matter either way just as long as it was done before we left this beautiful island." We did a little more shopping then retired to our suite. Even though we wanted to make love we decided to stop having sex until we got married and set the date for next fall. I couldn't wait to finally be his wife and mother of his child.

Isaac and I were on our way to Chicago to see Dr. Mariner. He was the best in his field and said he shouldn't have any problems reversing Isaac's vasectomy. I thought he told me he got the irreversible kind. He admitted to me he wanted to do that at first but decided to change it right before the procedure.

Ever since then, Mama had been a gem. She cooked us dinner twice a week and even took the kids shopping. Angela loved her to death because she told it like it was. I guessed they had the talk and now Angela had been asking me all about boys and what she was supposed to do about liking one in her class. I wasn't ready for that and wanted to tell Mama off for discussing it with her until she told me that Angela said she was scared to talk to me about it.

I couldn't understand why she was scared, but Mama said she felt like since I knew about the rape that I would think she was being fast. But she couldn't deny how she was changing physically and emotionally. Being a teenager was going to be tough. I'd been there before. I decided not to tell Isaac about it yet; he had enough on his mind.

Now we were about to go into the doctor's office before the procedure. Dr. Mariner asked him a lot of questions. The one that stuck out the most was why he decided to reverse the procedure. Isaac told him about my mom, but the doctor was not very uplifting.

He told us that even though the procedure was being reversed we had a long hill to climb toward pregnancy. There was only a fifty percent chance of reproduction after the reversal and only if the reversal was done within ten years of the procedure. That was probably the only thing we had going for us. He had the procedure done less than two years ago.

They wheeled Isaac into the outpatient surgery and about three hours later he was in recovery. We were going to stay in Chicago for two days to let him heal a little before getting back on the road. When we finally got back to Columbus, Mama had a big dinner waiting for us. I was shocked but happy to see her with so much hope in her heart again.

While he was coming downstairs, my mother stopped him at the bottom and gave him a hug and kiss on the cheek. He started to blush, but she was ecstatic. I could see a trace of tears in her eyes and the kids giggled. My family was coming together right before my eyes and in about three weeks, Isaac and I would officially begin our quest to have a baby. I loved my life, and I owed it all to God.

If He was not the head of my life, I wouldn't be in the place I was right now. His grace was sufficient, and His mercy endured forever. Now all I needed to do was go see an obstetrician and make sure I was fertile. This would be an uphill battle, but I knew we would be satisfied in Jesus in the end.

I decided to call Regina and check in with her a couple of days after we came back from Chicago.

"How did it go in the Bahamas?" I asked, expecting the worst.

"If you must know, I am now officially engaged to Jeremy Marquis Spencer. We shall be wed in October, and I will be the adopted mother of Jeremy Jr. within six months of our marriage. So there." She touted proudly.

"Well alright then. He finally grew up and put on his big boy shoes. It's about doggone time. I swear I thought I was going to have to beat him upside the head soon." I giggled with her.

"I know right. How have you been sis?"

"I've been blessed. You know we went to Chicago last week and he got his vasectomy reversed. The procedure went well but we can't have sex for another three weeks. And girl I can't wait. But the shock of the century his how your auntie Delores, my mama, has been acting ever since the man decided to do this. She has just about fallen in love with him now. I can hardly make him a meal without her coming over here with a plate of something. I'm starting to get jealous."

"That is too funny. But God is good. Too bad it had to take something so drastic to happen before she finally started accepting him. What are the doctors saying about the cancer?"

"She's still in chemo. She's been shopping for wigs online and keeps sending me pictures to help her pick out some. I don't care what happens, she is going to be a flawless, AKA a diva no matter what."

"That's good, she has a lot of hope and that is the best thing for her. But I gotta go, my fiancé is waiting on me."

"Y'all better not be getting down and dirty. It is better to wait now. It'll make the wedding night even more explosive."

"We know this, thank you."

"Girl, get off my phone." We hung up on each other and went back to our lives with our loved ones.

CHAPTER TWENTY

Let us pray?

Crystal

After all was said and prayed, we were living the lives we knew we were destined to live. I found out that I was indeed fertile and after trying for about two months, I was now seven weeks pregnant. Isaac said we couldn't tell anyone until I was three months. I wanted to at least tell my mother. She lost her hair and was feeling horrible.

The chemo was taking a toll on her. She seemed so weak now. It was like the cure was killing her worse than the disease itself. But she was a fighter. I knew she was going to get through this valley and come out on top. She had to; she was my mama, and she could do anything.

I was on pins and needles because I didn't know how to keep a secret, especially a secret this big. I was worried about Mama though. She didn't have that spark in her eyes anymore. Yesterday she laid in the bed again and had been doing that for almost a week. She only got up to go the bathroom and hadn't washed her tail in a long time.

When I walked into the house, I smelled a funk that I hadn't smelled since Daddy died. It took her months to get out of that funk and I didn't want her to become depressed over this as well. Her best friend Sharon was always checking up on her and being supportive. Some of her sorority sisters called and stopped by too. She had a whole community of people supporting her, so she had to fight this demon.

I couldn't take it anymore. She had to get up out of that bed. I marched upstairs, ready for the fight we were sure to have. I didn't care if we argued all night. She was getting out of that bed.

"Mama, please get up out of that bed," I demanded. It was the first time I ever outright demanded her to do something, and it felt good. I pulled the blanket off her.

She sprang up and said, "Girl who you do you think you are talking to? I am still your mother even though you have your own two now. I'm not feeling too good today, Keisha, leave me alone." She pulled the blankets back over her head and laid back down, exhausted.

"Mama, you gotta fight this illness. You can't just lay there and die on me. I won't let you." I started opening the curtains to let the sun in. I opened the window slightly to let some air in the room then started to take the blankets off her again.

"Stop Keisha! I mean it. I don't want to get out of bed. I deserve this."

"No, you don't. Stop saying that. You are a good woman and mother. Look at us; even my older siblings are all doing alright. I know we don't communicate much but we are all doing fine. And don't forget the ladies of AKA. That chapter wouldn't know what to do without you, and the church, remember the church, Mama. What would pastor do without your greens every Friday? The ladies of Zion wouldn't know how to take charge of themselves and everything that goes on in their lives without your example. Now you gotta get up. Get up Mama!" I shouted while pulling her out of the bed.

She started to whimper but did what I said because she knew I was not playing with her today. I knew she was sick, and the chemotherapy was taking its toll on her, but she could not lay there and die. I wouldn't let her. Delores Renee Mosley was a woman of great faith and power, no devil in hell was going to bind her up with this disease. I wouldn't let it happen, so I was putting the devil on notice, get thee behind me.

I drew a nice bath for her with some Epsom salt and then helped her get undressed. I let her cry because I couldn't remember the last time she cried. It may have been after Daddy died. That was a long time to hold back tears. But like the word said, He would bottle up every tear. She would live and not die, that was my declaration and decree.

Jeremy and I had been planning for our wedding and trying to stay chaste. I called the church and told them to put us on the calendar for October. We'd been waiting for a long time so there was no reason to prolong the engagement. Everything was going fine until I heard one of the sopranos talking about me in the bathroom after choir practice.

"Girl, I heard she had to give him an ultimatum. You know she's basic; ain't no man really wants to get with her," the girl said. Her face turned white when she saw me walk out of the stall. She never spoke to me, and I knew she was one of Cassandra's mean friends.

Cassandra had been my arch enemy since I was in high school. She always competed with me when there really was no competition. She might have been prettier with weave all down her back, but I was a class act. She'd been after Jeremy for years, following him like a puppy. Pathetic, and when we started dating, she lost it.

I knew we were going to have to have it out. It looked like today was going to be the day too, because here she came with the girl who was gossiping about me.

"Excuse me, may I speak with you in private please?"

"We don't have anything to talk about, Regina. Why do you want to talk to me?"

"I heard your little peon here spreading a rumor I know you started. Let me say this. I am marrying Jeremy Marquis Spencer in less than six months whether you like it or not. You lost girl, get over it. He was never going to be with you because you are trifling. Why would you want to be a preacher's wife when you don't know how to be humble and are way too much of a diva? Listen, grow up and get some help, really." I walked away like a boss before she could say anything. She was left standing there with her mouth open in total disbelief, but I knew I wouldn't have any more problems with her after that.

Now all I had to do was concentrate on this new opportunity to teach at Capital University. I had a bachelor's degree in mathematics and could teach college math. They need a new adjunct professor in the math department for their summer courses. I'd already applied for it and now I was waiting for the acceptance.

Later that night, I met with Jeremy, and we went over our guest list. It was going to be short. I wanted to have the wedding at the Kelton House where Keisha had her reception. I knew it was bad to have your wedding at the same place your best friend had her reception, but I loved the garden there. In early October the weather would be majestic as the leaves started to change and the temperature would be okay for me to wear a short-sleeved gown. I might decide to get a strapless one just to whip my hair back and forth.

I was getting married to the man I'd loved from day one. He was slow to move us along, but we were here now because of God. *Thank you for your grace and mercy, Lord, as it has followed me all the days of my life.* Now I could get on to being Mrs. Spencer.

CHAPTER TWENTY-ONE

Over the rainbow

Janet Crystal Ervin

I found the dress of my dreams to meet my man at the altar. As soon as I found it, I called my girl Keisha to meet me at the dress shop in Dublin. She got here as quickly as she could, and I tried it on again so she could see me in all my glory.

"Oh my God, Regina. Girl, you look stunning. If you don't get this dress, I am going to bop you upside the head. Jeremy is going to melt when he sees you."

"For real girl. I look that good in it?"

"Yes, you do. That's the one, that's your wedding gown." The dress was an off the shoulder antique white mermaid with a train made of chiffon with some Swarovski crystals on the sleeves and train. Even though I wore a size twelve, I had to get it into a fourteen to make sure it would fit without any bunching in the wrong places. It made my figure almost look as good as a coke bottle. He was going to be crying his eyeballs out and slobbering at the same time.

I was in my element.

That was until the doggone nurse came in telling me she had to give me my shot. She messed up my bliss. I could still see me and Keisha at the dress shop looking fabulous in the mirrors. But I was really in a six by nine single room at the Twin Valley Behavioral Health on the west side of Columbus. I guessed one of my girls got too out of it and they sent me here to get back to normal. But what was normal for a person with multiple personality disorder?

All I knew was my real name was Crystal, and when I see that wench Regina, I was going to beat her tail like she stole something. Here comes that quack doctor.

"So, Ms. Ervin, who are we today?"

"Doc don't come in here playing with me now. You know my name is Janet Crystal Ervin. How long have I been locked up in here?"

"After you tried to steal the wedding dress from David's bridal on Morse Road, I would have to say you have been here for about two weeks. But this is the first time I have been able to talk to the real you, Crystal. How are you feeling today?"

"Like a mouse trapped in a Ferris wheel."

"Tell me more about that feeling."

"Look, I ain't about to do all that. Just let me know when y'all are going to release me since I am finally back to myself. Where is my husband?"

"You don't have a husband, remember Crystal? Jeremy was a figment of your imagination and the other alter, Regina's beau."

"Okay, but who's taking care of little Chasity? Don't tell me that crackhead Barbara is. Y'all, know she smoke crack, right?"

"Well, they are both one of your personalities and we spoke to them last week. They are fine. We want to know how Janet Crystal Ervin is doing today since we haven't heard from you in over seven years."

"What?"

"Yes, you haven't been to Twin Valley for over seven years, Ms. Ervin. What happened that made you sick this time?"

I sat there and pondered my life over the past seven years. I had been bouncing back and forth between my girls for all this time and didn't even realize it. Oh my God, I did not have a love divine with anyone, did I? It was all a ruse, a dream, a fantasy made up in my mind. I guessed what they said in Proverbs 15:26 was true: "the thoughts of the wicked are an abomination to the Lord; but the words of the pure are pleasant words." Father God am I really insane? Why did you make me this way? How am I gonna live a productive life with these doggone meds? They keep me fatigued all of the time. Then I have to stop taking them if I want to feel normal. What kind of love do you really have for the mentally ill, God? Jesus? Are you even real?

How in the world was I going to get out of the psych ward this time? Rainbows are so spectacular, if only I could see one right now and revel in its beauty. I didn't want to talk to Doctor Thomas anymore. He had taken me away from my bliss. These dang on meds were starting to work too. I was already sleepy. I just wanted to look at Jeremy's face one more time. Just one more time please, God, are you listening to me?

THE END

Mental Health Assistance

If you, your loved one, spouse or friend or even an enemy has any issues with their mental health, please take the time to gain understanding of how to obtain proper treatment for them. The best place to start would be NAMI, the National Alliance on Mental Illness. Please, do not call the police first, contact your local emergency mental health organization instead. They can come out and serve the person humanly and make sure they get the medical attention they need. You may save their life with one informed call.

More ways to Help:

National Suicide and Crisis Lifeline: 988 (Call. Chat. Text.)

National 24/7 Suicide Hotline: 1-800-SUICIDE (1-800-784-2433)

Military Veterans Suicide Hotline: 1-800-273-TALK (Press 1)

Suicide Hotline in Spanish: 1-800-273-TALK (Press 2)

LGBT Youth Suicide Hotline: 1-866-4-U-TREVOR

CRISIS TEXT LINE:

Text "4HOPE" to 741-741

Free, 24/7, Confidential: Crisis Text Line serves anyone in any type of crisis, providing them access to free, 24/7 emotional support and information they need via the medium they already use and trust: text. Here's how it works:

- Someone texts into Crisis Text Line anywhere, anytime, about any type of crisis.

- A live, trained specialist receives the text and responds quickly.

- The specialist helps the person stay safe and healthy with effective, secure counseling and referrals through text message using Crisis Text Line's platform.

Other Books Written by Toya Raylonn Vickers

Christian Fiction

Dimes, Profiles and Wives: Today's Proverbs 31 Woman (DPW)

Love Without a Limit: DPW Book 2

To Say I Do: DPW Book 3

Fool for Love: Devil in Disguise

Christian Non-Fiction

Coming Soon 2024-2026

Church Hurt: Don't Deny the Damage Done

From Pain to Purpose:
Battling the Untransformed Mind

My Name is Victory:
Chronicles of Toya Raylonn Vickers

One More Thing:

To my Fans and The Tribe

Thank you for supporting me since 2010. Thirteen years is a long time to remain relevant in this industry. If you want to have your book signed, send me a direct message on social media.

You all help me to remain sane! L.O.L..... but for real though.

A merry heart doeth good like medicine. Proverbs 17:22

Always,

Cookie's Daughter and Name Sake,

Toya Raylonn Vickers

December 23, 2023

Meet the Author

Toya Raylonn Vickers was born in Toledo, raised in Columbus, Ohio and currently lives in Dallas, Texas. She is an African American woman who loves writing. She holds a Bachelor of Arts degree in Psychology from The Ohio State University and matriculated at Howard University to gain a Master's in Social Work. In 2003, exactly two months before she was to graduate from Howard with top honors, she survived a disastrous car crash. Unable to walk and obtain the master's degree as Suma Cum Lade, she began writing again, a lost talent, while in her hospital bed at Howard University Hospital. After an almost six-month hospitalization she returned to Columbus, Ohio and began the long road to recovery, redemption, and reconciliation.

During her fight to gain her place in society she was diagnosed with a mental health disease. However, believing in Jesus Christ's strength and power as well as her mustard seed faith along with a bit of courage, she began the long road to healing. In 2006 after much prayer and fasting she returned to her talent of writing, authored her first novel Dimes, Profiles, and Wives (DPW) then published it with Xlibris in 2010. DPW was the first book of many to come from this author entrepreneur. She is a published poet, novice song writer, in addition she's the CEO and founder of ToyShelf Services LLC. She dares to walk in the newness of life and humbly writes to glorify God. She feels that even though her life has been filled with many obstacles she can still contribute to the world through writing. She hopes by this art form more people will come to know who God is, believe in His son, Jesus Christ, and live the most important commandment in the Holy Bible, John 13:34: A new commandment I give unto you, that ye love one another; as I have loved you, that ye also love one another.

Toya Raylonn's writing coach and mentor Joylynn Ross expressed:

> "Toya Vickers is an excellent example of a writer who started off with just a story to tell, but with her persistent hard work and dedication, transitioned into a talented author." - Joylynn M. Ross writing as BLESSEDselling Author E. N. Joy

The woman, Raylonn Smith and her first born
daughter and junior, Toya Raylonn Vickers.

Mama, I will always love you, thank you for loving me.